"Someone shot me," Ally whispered.

"Did you see who did this to you?" Tucker asked. He lifted her hand and he saw the bullet wound, then pressed her hand back and put his own pressure on it.

She grimaced, but shook her head. "No, I didn't see anyone."

"Help is on the way," he assured her. "You're going to be okay. What are you doing here?"

She breathed through a burst of pain. "I was searching for my mother. She went missing here twenty years ago. This was the last place she was seen. I believe she was murdered here."

A murder at his family's ranch? Tucker didn't remember anything about that. Yet, Ally had come here to investigate her mother's disappearance and now she'd been shot?

It was too much of a coincidence to ignore. Someone was targeting Ally, as well...

Virginia Vaughan is a born-and-raised Mississippi girl. She is blessed to come from a large Southern family, and her fondest memories include listening to stories recounted around the dinner table. She was a lover of books from a young age, devouring tales of romance, danger and love. She soon started writing them herself. You can connect with Virginia through her website, virginiavaughanonline.com, or through the publisher.

Books by Virginia Vaughan

Love Inspired Suspense

Cowboy Protectors

Kidnapped in Texas
Texas Ranch Target
Dangerous Texas Hideout
Texas Ranch Cold Case

Cowboy Lawmen

Texas Twin Abduction
Texas Holiday Hideout
Texas Target Standoff
Texas Baby Cover-Up
Texas Killer Connection
Texas Buried Secrets

Visit the Author Profile page at LoveInspired.com for more titles.

Texas Ranch Cold Case

VIRGINIA VAUGHAN

LOVE INSPIRED SUSPENSE

INSPIRATIONAL ROMANCE

LOVE INSPIRED® SUSPENSE
INSPIRATIONAL ROMANCE

ISBN-13: 978-1-335-59961-2

Texas Ranch Cold Case

Recycling programs for this product may not exist in your area.

Love Inspired
22 Adelaide St. West, 41st Floor
Toronto, Ontario M5H 4E3, Canada
www.LoveInspired.com

Printed in Lithuania

MIX
Paper | Supporting responsible forestry
FSC® C021394

And whatsoever ye do in word or deed,
do all in the name of the Lord Jesus,
giving thanks to God and the Father by him.
—*Colossians* 3:17

The Christian fiction community lost two great readers and encouragers during the time I was writing this story—Susan Snodgrass and Caron Tweet. Both were members of my review team and wonderfully encouraging women of Christ. This book is dedicated to their memories and their love of reading.

ONE

This is impossible.

Ally Fulton pushed away that negative thought. Lush, green pasture stretched out in front of her for as far as she could see. Her task did seem overwhelming, but what else could she do? She'd been stymied in her search for her missing mother on all sides since coming to Jessup, Texas, and given that she'd found no evidence her mother had left here when she'd vanished, Ally was convinced her body was buried somewhere among the green hills of Harmon Ranch.

She parked her ATV, climbed off and pulled out her map. She'd found the land map online and sketched out a grid she could mark off one by one. It was a massive job, but one she was committed to doing…at least until something else broke on her mother's case.

Twenty years.

That was how long Tonya Fulton had been

missing and no one else was even searching for her. Ally had always wondered about what had happened to her mom, but her aunt had encouraged her not to obsess over her disappearance. However, when her aunt had died and Ally discovered she'd been conducting her own investigation into Tonya's disappearance, Ally had picked up where she'd left off, coming to Jessup eight months ago to try to find answers. But she'd been stopped at every turn. She hadn't been able to get the files from the Jessup Police Department to discover what had been done on the case and the detective she'd spoken with at the police station had insisted they couldn't release the records since it was technically an open investigation.

Of course, it was an open investigation. No one was working to close it.

So this was what she was relegated to. Searching a 5,000-acre ranch for her mother's body on a Monday afternoon.

She pulled out her metal detector. In every memory she had of her mother, she'd always worn a locket with Ally's baby picture inside. It wasn't a guarantee that wherever she was, she was still wearing it, but again, it was a start. And it was all she had.

Frustration riddled her as she began walking along with the metal detector skimming the ground. The steady beep mocked her. *Silly, Ally. You already have the answers you need. You only have to remember.*

That was the problem. She'd been with her mother the day she'd vanished only, even all these years later, she still had no memory of what had happened on that terrible day.

She'd knocked on every door she could think of, from the local police station to the state attorney general's office. She'd even sent a letter to the governor begging for help, but the Harmon name carried a lot of weight in the state of Texas. No one was going to go against Chet Harmon. She'd tried to contact him, only to have his lawyers shut her down with a cease-and-desist letter. Her mother had worked at Harmon Ranch when she'd gone missing and possibly even been in a relationship with him. He'd held the answers she'd needed to solve her mother's disappearance, yet his influence in this town and in this state had thwarted all of Ally's efforts to find answers. Now, Chet Harmon had died and taken the truth to his grave. He would never give her the information she sought, so she was left with no choice but to conduct her own search.

The hot Texas sun barreled down on her and she wiped away sweat. Summer was fast approaching and these searches would get worse as the months inched by.

A noise caught her attention and she spun around, her pulse ramping up. A critter skittered by. Ally breathed out a sigh of relief. She didn't have permission to be on Harmon Ranch and she doubted she would be welcomed, but she'd told herself the land was so massive that no one would even know she was there.

Suddenly, the birds fluttered and a shot rang out. Ally screamed as pain ripped through her arm. She fell to the ground at the force of the bullet that had hit her.

Fear surged through her as another shot was fired, this one whizzing past her, barely missing.

Someone was shooting at her.

A terrible thought raced through her. She was going to vanish on Harmon Ranch, just as her mother had.

Tucker Harmon pulled his horse to a stop and took in a deep breath. He'd missed the fresh air and views of his grandfather's massive Texas ranch.

He hadn't been here in years and had hesitated in even returning after falling out with his grandfather. Now, Chet Harmon was dead and Tucker was more than a little surprised to learn that he'd left him, and his three other cousins, a share of the ranch.

It had taken months to get him here. He'd sworn never to set foot on Harmon Ranch again, but things had changed three weeks ago, when he'd led a SWAT raid that went sideways.

The images of the terrified little girl and her mom flashed through his mind. Her boyfriend had taken them both hostage. Tucker had fired a shot and killed the boyfriend, but not before the man had squeezed off several shots, including one that hit Tucker and another that had ended the girlfriend's life.

He grimaced and rubbed the shoulder where one of those bullets had landed. His wound was healing but the aftermath of the incident had turned ugly when the murderer's wealthy father had flexed his political muscles and blamed Tucker solely for his son's death. Tucker had been through all the reports and inquiries about the incident and, even though it was still under investigation, he'd yet to be cleared of any wrongdoing. Tucker was to be the department's scapegoat. At least, that was how it had felt when his supervisor had placed him on indefinite medical leave.

He turned his horse and urged him on before he got too lost in his own thoughts. After that incident, he'd wanted a place to hide out. This was what he needed to get his head clear. Room to roam, fresh air and no memories of murder.

A shot rang out, then a scream. He yanked on the reins, pulling the horse to a stop. He scanned the area. The sound had come from the east, toward the back side of the property. He pushed the horse in that direction and kicked him into a gallop. Tucker heard a hum then spotted an ATV moving fast in the opposite direction. The sun glared off the rider's helmet, blinding him to the driver's identity.

He kept going, stopping when he spotted a woman stumbling toward him. She was holding her shoulder, and even from this distance, he could see blood pooling around her fingers.

He pulled the horse to a stop and leaped from it just as she stumbled to the ground. He ran to her. She was pale and her shirt was turning red with blood. Not a good sign.

"Ma'am, are you okay?" Of course, he could see she wasn't, but he needed to get her talking if possible. Keep her conscious while he assessed her injuries.

"I've been shot." She whispered the words and even then they were filled with pain and anguish.

"Did you see who did this to you?" He lifted her hand and saw the bullet wound, then pressed her hand back and put his own pressure on it.

She grimaced in pain at the added pressure but shook her head. "No, I didn't see anyone. I heard the shot then nearly passed out from the pain."

He grabbed his cell phone and dialed for help. She needed to go to a hospital for treatment before she bled out, but an ambulance would take forever. He phoned the barn instead and waited for Ed Lance, the ranch manager, to pick up. He should also remember to call his cousin Caleb, who was the chief of police in town.

The barn phone rang six times and Tucker nearly hung up before Ed answered. "Harmon Ranch." He sounded out of breath, like he'd run to answer. As a nearly seventy-year-old man, he usually left the hard work to the ranch hands and spent most of his days overseeing and pushing papers in his office inside the barn.

"Ed, I'm out by the old hay shed on the east side of the property. I need a truck. A woman has been shot. She needs to get to the hospital." There was no way he could get her onto the horse and, with her injury, she wouldn't be able to climb very well.

"I'm on my way," Ed told him, then hung up.

"Help is on the way," he assured the woman. "You're going to be okay."

He wasn't going to let another woman die in

front of him. He'd come here to get away from shootings and madmen and death.

"What's your name?"

"Ally. Ally Fulton."

"What are you doing here, Ally Fulton?"

She breathed through what looked like a burst of pain before answering him. "I was searching the grounds for my mother. She went missing here twenty years ago."

"Why do you think she's here?"

"This was the last place she was seen. She used to work for Chet Harmon."

Twenty years ago, he'd been a child, yet he'd spent a lot of time on the ranch. "Who was your mother?"

"Tonya Fulton. She was Chet Harmon's bookkeeper before she vanished. I believe she was murdered here."

A murder at Harmon Ranch? He didn't remember anything about that. Yet, she'd come to Harmon Ranch to investigate her mother's disappearance and now she'd been shot?

It was too much of a coincidence to ignore.

Someone had targeted Ally Fulton and Tucker had seen the perpetrator scurrying away.

He checked her wound again and tried to clean it up with a bandanna from his saddlebag. He tied it around her arm, doing his best to stop the bleeding. "Keep pressing your hand against that," he told her. He glanced at his phone. Ed seemed to be taking forever and her color was still off. He didn't know if it was from blood loss, the shock of being shot or both, but she needed to get to the hospital. "Do you think you can stay on the horse?"

She glanced at it and worry colored her expression. "I'm not sure. My ATV is over the hill." She dug into her pocket then frowned. "I must have dropped the key."

He helped her to her feet. She was petite, only five-four or so, and he thought he could lift her onto the horse. "I'm going to help you up but use your good arm to climb on." He held the horse and her steady, then cupped his hands for her to place her foot into. He heaved her up and she climbed onto the horse. He made certain she was balanced before climbing on, too.

"You okay? Hold on to me."

Tucker turned the horse and nudged it back toward the barn. She clutched his waist with her good arm and leaned into him. He could smell sweat and a strawberry scent—probably from her shampoo—and it tickled his nose. It was a good thing he'd been out this way. He didn't know how she would have made it back on her own, especially without her keys.

A hum caught his ear as they rode. It sounded like the motor he'd heard from the ATV speeding away after Ally had been shot. He tensed and scanned the area, but relaxed a bit when he saw a vehicle approaching. Ed. Finally.

He drew the horse to a stop as Ed pulled up close to them and cut the engine.

"Tucker, what's happening?"

"We decided to meet you halfway," Tucker said, hopping from the horse. He held out his arms to help Ally to the ground. She was much lighter coming off the horse than getting onto it.

Ed climbed out of the truck. "What happened to you, young lady?"

"Someone shot her," Tucker responded. "Out on the east ridge. Send some guys out there to have a look for anything suspicious." He walked Ally around to the passenger's side, then opened the door and helped her in before circling back to Ed. "Can you take the horse back to the barn? I'm going to borrow your truck to take Ally to the hospital." He climbed behind the wheel before Ed could even give him a "yeah, sure."

"I'll call Caleb and let him know what's happening."

"Thanks, Ed." Tucker started the engine, turned the truck around, then took off.

"Caleb?" Ally asked.

"My cousin Caleb. He's kind of in charge at the ranch since my grandfather died. He's also the chief of police here in Jessup. He'll want to know what happened."

"That makes two of us," she said wistfully.

"Don't worry," he told her. "We'll figure this out."

He wanted answers, too. She'd come searching for a missing mother only to be shot on his newly inherited property.

Ally groaned in pain as the nurse bandaged her wound. The bullet had grazed her arm and she'd bled a lot, but it wasn't a serious injury. She was thankful she wouldn't have to have surgery, although the doctor had told her she would be in pain for a while.

She needed to keep moving it to prevent it from growing stiff.

She had no intention of sitting around holding her arm. This had been no accident. Someone had shot her for trying to locate her mother's body.

The door opened and a man wearing a police uniform, boots and a cowboy hat entered her room. Following behind him was the man who'd saved her life. She hadn't had time to really examine him, but she did now. Tall and handsome with thick dark hair and a hint of a beard. He stood a head taller than his cousin and was broader. He held his cowboy hat in his hands and his eyes scanned her before he flashed her a careful smile.

"You look better."

"Thank you. I don't feel very well, though."

"It could have been worse."

Didn't she know it. For a moment, she'd had visions of herself disappearing in the vast open space of Harmon Ranch. Only, unlike her mother, she had no one who would have come searching for her.

"This is my cousin Caleb. He's the police chief. I told him what happened and he needs to get your statement."

She used her good arm to try to push herself to a better sitting position. "Sure."

Caleb pulled out a pen and notebook. "My cousin has already given me his version. Why don't you tell me what happened in your own words, starting with why you were out there?"

Why were you trespassing on private property? She saw the question in his eyes although his presentation was more tactful.

"I came to Jessup eight months ago. Since that time, I've been trying to find out what happened to my mother. She went missing and no one has ever found her."

"And you think she's somewhere on the ranch?"

She shrugged. "It's the last place she was seen and her body has never been recovered."

"What was she doing at Harmon Ranch to begin with?"

"She worked there. She was a bookkeeper. Her name was Tonya Fulton."

"I don't recognize the name. Our accountant is Bill Collins. How long ago was this?"

"Twenty years."

He lowered his notebook. "Your mother has been missing for twenty years and you thought you could find her on a 5,000-acre ranch with an ATV and a metal detector?"

Her face warmed. She knew how ridiculous it sounded but that was how desperate she was for answers. "I know it's unlikely but I'd run out of options. I had to do something. I haven't been able to get any of the official police records because Detective Martin told me that it was an open case and that no records could be released to the public." She bit her tongue before she reminded them it was still open because no one was working it.

Tucker glanced at his cousin. "Have you ever heard of this case?"

Caleb shook his head. "Never. I have a list of cold cases back at my office. I'll look but I don't recognize the name."

"That still doesn't explain who shot you

today," Tucker said. "I saw someone racing off but didn't get a look at them. Any idea who would want to hurt you?"

Whoever killed my mother and doesn't want me investigating. "I don't know. Maybe someone who didn't want me on the property?" She gave them both a hard glare, but neither faltered under it.

Caleb rubbed the back of his neck. "I don't appreciate you trespassing on the property without permission, but I find it hard to believe anyone at the ranch would take a shoot-first-and-ask-questions-later stance. We haven't had any reason to be wary of trespassers—at least, not very recently. Is there anyone in your life that holds a grudge against you or might want to harm you?"

"No. No one. I'm a teacher at the middle school and I've only been in town for less than a year. I've hardly had time to make any enemies."

"What about boyfriends?"

"I'm not in a relationship."

"Ex-boyfriends?"

She'd dated some but all her relationships had ended amicably. "No. There's no one."

"And you didn't see anyone as you were performing your search?"

She shook her head. "I didn't see anyone. I

heard an ATV but before I could see where it was, I was shot. The only other person I saw was Tucker."

"And you didn't shoot her, right?" Caleb asked him.

Tucker glared at his cousin a moment before responding. "No, I didn't shoot her. I wasn't even armed."

"Okay then, I'll talk to the ranch employees. Maybe someone there saw or heard something that might identify this person. In the meantime, I'll have Ed send out a group to check over every square inch of the ranch for other intruders. I'd hate to think someone might be using our property for nefarious reasons."

Ally breathed out a sigh of relief. She hadn't even considered that possibility. Harmon Ranch was a large, isolated area. Maybe someone was performing criminal activity and she'd gotten too close so they'd tried to frighten her off.

She relaxed a little, not even realizing that she'd been on guard since the moment of being shot at. She'd automatically blamed the Harmon Ranch owners, even though one of them had saved her and the other was just trying to do his job.

"Well, thankfully, the bullet only grazed me. It bled a lot and it hurts but I'll survive."

Caleb put away his notebook. "Unless you

can give me more information, I'll let you get some rest. I'd recommend not going out there alone until we figure this out."

He wasn't exactly telling her not to continue her investigation, but she wanted to make them both aware that she wasn't giving up the search for her mom, despite today's incident. "I came to Jessup to find answers about my mother's disappearance. I realize it's risky but I still need to find out what happened to her. I won't give up."

Tucker glanced at his cousin, then back at her. "I understand your need to find answers but you shouldn't risk your own life to do so."

She locked eyes with Tucker, who matched her gaze. "What else am I supposed to do? Someone killed my mother and I intend to find out who did it and what happened to her."

Their grandfather had been a powerful figure in Jessup and in Texas. Someone knew what had happened to her mom and, from what she'd heard, nothing happened at Harmon Ranch without Chet Harmon's knowledge. He could have found answers for her, but he hadn't. Instead, he'd hidden the truth from her then died with the answers she needed still a secret.

She was going to find out the truth and she wouldn't allow anyone, especially anyone named Harmon, to stand in her way.

* * *

Tucker followed his cousin down the hospital corridor. "What do you think?"

Caleb didn't miss a beat. "I think it's a hopeless search. Even if her mother was killed and buried at the ranch, she'll have a hard time uncovering it after twenty years."

"Agreed. I don't remember anything about a murder at the ranch twenty years ago."

"Neither do I, but we were just kids back then."

"We were old enough to remember something like that happening. I have no memory of this woman working at the ranch, or her daughter." Twenty years ago, he would have been eleven years old, but by then, he wasn't spending much time at the ranch. As he recalled, it wouldn't have been long since his father had died, so the activities on the ranch wouldn't have been close to his mind. "What about the fact that she hasn't gotten any information from your office?"

Caleb stopped and turned to him. "This is the first I've heard about it. She said she spoke to Detective Martin. I'll ask him, but if it is still an open investigation, he's not wrong that he can't share it."

"It's a decades-old cold case. I would think

some information could be released to the family."

Caleb shrugged. "I'll look into it and see what I can find. What are you going to do?"

Tucker didn't know exactly but he had to do something. "Try to find out more about what's going on with her. Maybe, like you said, she stumbled across something going on at the ranch, or this is something to do with her personal life and she doesn't even realize it."

Caleb looked at him worriedly. "You don't have to do that. You're in town to relax and heal, not to delve into a stranger's problems."

"I know I don't have to, but she seems so alone. I guess I know what that feels like."

Caleb nodded then walked away.

Tucker couldn't explain his desire to offer his assistance to the pretty schoolteacher. He only knew that he recognized someone in trouble when he saw it and he wanted to help if he could.

Ally phoned her supervisor to explain what had happened and let her know that she might need a substitute for her class for a day or two. She wasn't badly injured but the pain was already significant and she wanted to let her co-workers prepare in case she needed significant time to recover.

The nurse was readying her to check out when the door to her room opened and another teacher in her school, Jenny Summers, entered carrying a vase of flowers. Ally's and Jenny's classes were both on the same hallway at the middle school and they'd become friends chatting during the class changes and breaks.

Jenny carried the vase of flowers into the room. "When Principal Shorter said you'd been shot, I expected to find you in a hospital bed hooked up to machines. You look good."

She took the flowers from Jenny and smelled them before setting the vase on the end table. "Thank you. It only grazed me. I think it was more scary than anything else." She held up her sleeve to show Jenny the bandage.

Jenny's eyes widened at the sight of the bandage. "Ally, what happened?"

She pulled down her sleeve. "I was performing a search for my mother when someone shot me."

Jenny's eyes widened again. "Ally, you have to be more careful." Jenny was the only one Ally had told about why she'd really moved to Jessup at the beginning of the school year.

A tear welled up in her eye and she wiped it away. "I can't just do nothing. I owe my mother's memory more than that."

"I know you do but trespassing on the Harmon Ranch is dangerous in and of itself. That family practically runs this town. Everyone knows it."

She knew it, too. All the avenues to finding answers about her mother had been blocked by Chet Harmon. Now that he was dead, his family name and influence were still making things difficult for her.

"You'd better hope they don't find you trespassing on their ranch. You'll have bigger trouble."

Ally's face warmed. "Actually, Tucker Harmon is the one who rescued me."

Her friend's eyes widened again. "Tucker Harmon? I'd heard he returned to town. What was he like?"

She recalled his gentle manner as he'd tended to her arm, then helped her onto the horse. "He was nice. He called his cousin Caleb to the hospital, too."

"You met the chief?"

"I did. I got the impression he didn't know about my mom's case but he said he would look into it. I'm not holding my breath but at least I got their attention."

"Sure, but by almost dying."

"I didn't almost die, Jenny. The bullet barely grazed me." The pain in her arm belied that statement at just that moment. She grabbed her arm and winced.

Jenny saw and gave her a knowing smile. "Being shot is serious, Ally. Someone didn't want you poking around asking questions. Do you think they're trying to stop you from digging into your mother's case?"

She had. At first. "Caleb suggested there might have been trespassers on the property that I might have gotten too close to and they were the ones who shot at me. It was just a theory but it makes sense. Who else even knew I was there? I went right after school and didn't tell anyone I was going."

"I don't know, but I hope you'll be careful in the future."

The nurse entered with her discharge papers.

"Just in time," Jenny stated. "I assume you don't have your car. I'll drive you home."

"Thank you, Jenny." Her car was still parked on the side of the road, along with the trailer she'd used to transport the ATV onto the Harmon property. And her keys were probably lost somewhere out in the field.

Ally hurried up and changed from hospital attire into her regular clothes. The nurse handed her the discharge papers along with prescriptions for painkillers and antibiotics.

"You take care of yourself, hon," the nurse

told her. "And come back if you see any signs of infection."

"I will. Thank you."

Jenny drove her home, where Ally saw her car parked in her driveway along with the ATV and trailer she'd left at Harmon Ranch. She'd wondered how she was going to get it back but it seemed someone had taken care of it already.

Tucker. It must have been him. He was the only one she could think of that knew the ATV belonged to her.

Jenny parked. "I assume you're taking a few days off from work?"

"I'm not sure yet. I might feel fine tomorrow. I'm playing it by ear."

"You really should take some time off. We can cover for you." Jenny sighed as she looked at her. "But I know how stubborn you can be. Call me if you need anything."

Ally thanked her then got out. She didn't have her keys so she entered the code to open the garage. She could enter the house through that door since she rarely locked it. She turned to wave as Jenny backed out of the driveway, then she lowered the garage door and went inside. Home was a three-bedroom ranch-style home, small but suitable for just her needs. She'd purchased it with the money she'd received after selling her aunt's house.

She stopped at the mantel and stared at a framed photograph of her aunt Kay and her mom when they were younger. She had only a few vague recollections of her mother. Most of her memories had been wiped away by trauma, the good ones taken along with the bad, but she had the stories Aunt Kay had told her through the years.

Her aunt had also advised her not to let her missing mother's case become an obsession for her, but how could it not?

She'd discovered so much since Aunt Kay had died in a car wreck two years ago. She'd learned of her aunt's secret obsession with her sister's disappearance and the fact that Chet Harmon had supported Kay and Ally for most of Ally's life. He'd even purchased the home they'd lived in and paid for Ally's schooling.

What kind of man did that for a missing employee's daughter?

She set the photograph back on the mantel. She knew the answer to that.

A guilty man.

Chet Harmon had died and taken his secrets to the grave, but Ally was intent on digging them all up and exposing them, no matter the cost.

TWO

The next morning, Tucker dressed, then headed downstairs. The house was quiet but he heard voices as he approached the kitchen. He found Hannah, the Harmon Ranch housekeeper for as long as he could remember, sitting at the table with Penny, Caleb's wife, and her little girl, Missy.

"Good morning," he said as he poured himself a cup of coffee.

"Good morning," Penny replied.

"Morning." Hannah stood. "Want me to make you some breakfast?"

"No, thanks. I'm not hungry." He wasn't used to having someone cooking and cleaning for him. He was used to taking care of himself and, although, he liked Hannah and had good memories of her, having her hovering over him was a little unsettling.

Thankfully, she had Caleb, Penny and Missy to keep her busy.

Penny wiped her daughter's mouth then shooed her from the table. "Go brush your teeth and grab your backpack. I'll drive you to school."

Hannah grabbed a lunchbox that was so stuffed it was straining the zipper. "I packed you your favorite peanut-butter-and-apple-jelly sandwich."

Missy took the lunchbox then hugged Hannah. "Thank you, Hannah. I'll see you after school."

"You're picking her up today, right?" Penny reminded Hannah. "I'm working the afternoon shift at the bakery." She put her hand on her stomach and Tucker noticed her swollen belly.

"I'll pick her up from school. Don't worry. I won't forget."

The mother-and-daughter duo hurried from the kitchen and Tucker heard them outside climbing into a car. He noticed Hannah was all smiles as she watched them.

"She and Caleb are having a baby?" he asked. He hadn't heard that news yet, but it was obvious.

"They are. They're having a little girl."

"They seem nice," Tucker said as Hannah began clearing the breakfast dishes.

"They are. I'm so happy they're here. After

Luke and Abby moved out, this big house would have seemed so empty again."

One of his other cousins, Luke, a retired FBI agent, had recently moved his wife and two kids to Dallas to work in their cousin Brett's security firm.

"But that little girl keeps me busy and I can't wait for the baby to arrive. I love Penny, too, and she's good for Caleb. They both are. They make him happy so that makes me happy." She touched Tucker's arm as she passed by him. "I'd like to see you happy like that, too, one day."

Hannah had always been a grandmotherly figure to him…to them all. It had been nice when he was a kid, but being away from the ranch for so long, he wasn't sure how to reclaim those soft feelings for her or anyone else here at Harmon Ranch.

His grandfather had inspired loyalty in his staff, something he hadn't been able to do for his own family. Perhaps that was because he tended to treat his staff better. Tucker's dad had died when he was ten and Chet Harmon had all but abandoned him and his mother since that day. She'd been forced to marry Dave Mathis, a hard man with violent tendencies who'd made both Tucker and his mother's lives a nightmare until Tucker was old enough to get out on his own.

Taking care of himself had become a necessary skill for survival.

For some reason, that made him think of Ally Fulton.

He leaned against the counter as he bit into a piece of toast. "Hannah, you've been here at Harmon Ranch for a long time, haven't you?"

She'd gotten busy loading the dishwasher. "Sure have. Going on thirty-five years."

"Then you would remember a woman who worked here. Tonya Fulton."

She stopped and glanced at him, an obvious look of recognition on her face. "Yes, I remember her." She shook her head. "Tragic what happened to her. She just up and vanished one day. Some people say she ran off, but she would never have left that little girl behind. Why are you asking about her?"

"Her daughter, Ally, is back in town."

Hannah stopped and tilted her head as if searching for a memory. "Come to think of it, I had heard she'd moved to town last year when we were all still dealing with your grandfather's death. I guess I had forgotten about her being here."

"I found her yesterday on the east side of the ranch. Someone shot her."

Surprise crossed Hannah's face. "Oh, my. Is she okay?"

"Yes, the bullet only grazed her. Tell me about what happened to Tonya."

She turned to finish filling up the dishwasher. "There isn't much to tell. She was a sweet lady. I remember she had a close relationship with your grandfather."

"Were they a couple?"

"Well, I don't know. There was quite an age difference between them but they were very close. I think your Grandpa Chet thought of her as a surrogate daughter. By that time, all of his kids had passed on, and you and your cousins weren't coming around the ranch as much as you used to."

Tucker didn't bother to remind her that his Grandpa Chet had been the one to push away Tucker and his cousins. He'd been so consumed with the loss of his four sons over a number of years that he'd allowed his grief to make him bitter and mean.

"Oh, and he loved that little girl, too. You know, they found her hiding inside a stall in the barn the day her mom disappeared. She was inconsolable."

"What exactly happened to Tonya? You said some people thought she ran off."

"That's just gossip. No one really knows. Well, that little girl probably does. We all felt like she must have seen what happened to her mother and was traumatized by it. She was hysterical. I'll never forget that look in her little eyes."

Ally hadn't mentioned that she'd been there when her mother had gone missing. "They never found her mother's body?"

"Not as far as I know."

"Did the police have any suspects at the time?"

She put her hand on her hip as she looked at him. "Not that I'm aware of. I think the consensus was that a wanderer must have come through and killed her, and buried her body so well that it was never found. I remember feeling frightened for months after that. I married my husband, Charlie, about a year later and was glad to move off the ranch."

Tucker vaguely remembered her wedding and had heard about her husband's death from cancer several years earlier. "I never gave you my condolences on Charlie's death."

"Thank you, Tucker. It was a difficult few years for me once he was gone, but I always had the ranch to come back to. This place has been my second home and everyone here my family. It was another blow when Chet died, but at least it's served to bring all you boys back to the ranch."

Tucker's dad had been Chet Harmon's third

child, of four sons. He'd lost all of them in a span of only a few years, each one leaving behind a son of his own—Tucker, Caleb, Luke and Brett. Now, they'd each returned to claim a fourth of the ranch as an inheritance.

"Where was Ally's father?"

Hannah shook her head. "I don't know. Tonya was a very private person. Of course, I'm sure there was gossip around town. Jessup is and was a small town. Tonya had been married once but her husband had died years before she started working at the ranch. She was here about six years before Ally was born. If she told anyone who the father was, it wasn't me."

"Do you think it was Grandpa Chet?" Was it possible the pretty woman he'd just met was his aunt?

"Not a chance. If she had been, Chet would have done right by her. He'd have married her and raised that child himself." Tucker had a difficult time believing in his grandfather's generosity. It was obviously something he'd saved for his employees because he certainly hadn't shared anything with Tucker or his mom. If he had, she wouldn't have had to marry Dave.

"What do you think happened to Tonya?" he asked Hannah.

She shook her head. "I wish I knew."

"Her daughter believes she has to be here on

the ranch buried somewhere. This was the last place she was seen alive."

"If she was, I'm sure the police would have found her back then."

"So they did search for her?"

"Of course. Why wouldn't they?"

Hannah had cared for his grandfather and had been loyal to him, so Tucker didn't just want to accuse him, but it was a known fact that most women were killed by their significant others. If Tonya and his grandfather had been in a relationship, Grandpa Chet had to be considered a suspect.

Only, he didn't have to voice his suspicions. She saw where his mind was going.

She shook her head, then slammed the dishwasher closed and started it. "No, Tucker. I know you don't have a great opinion of your Grandpa Chet, but he wasn't a killer. I don't know how serious their relationship was but he would never have harmed her."

"He was in a dark place back then, Hannah. He'd already lost three of his sons."

"I don't care. He wasn't like that." She glanced around, then wiped her hands nervously on her apron. "Now, if you'll excuse me, I have laundry to do." She walked out, her attention anywhere except on him, a distinct change from earlier in the conversation.

He took the hint. He'd gone too far. "I think I'll go see Caleb."

Tucker left the house, hopped into his pickup and drove to town. Jessup had grown and changed since he was a kid and he had to consult his GPS to find the police station.

He hadn't set out to upset Hannah and he was sorry he had, but listening to Ally's story had piqued something inside of him. She deserved to have answers to her questions about what had happened to her mother and it wasn't right that the truth was being withheld from her. He didn't suspect his cousin of any wrongdoing. He'd only been a kid, just like Tucker, when her mom went missing, but it wouldn't surprise him to learn that the Harmon influence had affected the case back then and possibly still did today.

If Chet Harmon had been involved in Tonya Fulton's disappearance, few people would have dared confront him about it.

It wasn't right for his grandfather's influence to deny her answers.

He parked and walked inside, and was greeted by a dispatcher who called to Caleb's office, then pointed the way to his office after getting the okay to do so.

Tucker was ashamed to admit he didn't know the way. He'd spent a lot of time in this town as a child but hadn't been back as an adult, even to visit with his cousins. His anger toward his grandfather had been too great. He'd never even considered returning until now and it had taken him a long time to even make the decision to come.

Chet Harmon had hung him out to dry as a child so Tucker had had no use for him as an adult.

He knocked on the door with Chief of Police on it and Caleb called him inside.

"Tucker, hey, what's up? What are you doing here?"

"Well, I was hoping to take a look at that case file on Ally Fulton's mother."

Caleb leaned against the desk. Tucker could see his request irritated him. "I told you, it's an open investigation. I can't have civilians—"

"I'm not a civilian. I'm a trained police officer just like you. In fact, I've probably worked more cases like this than you, given I work in a larger jurisdiction."

"You have investigative experience?"

His lack of knowledge was understandable. Tucker had been working SWAT for the last several years and before that, he hadn't spoken to any of his cousins since they were children. "I do. I trained as an investigator but I got tired of landing the cases when there was nothing I could do but clean up after the crime.

I transferred to SWAT in the hopes of getting the bad guys off the street and saving lives, but I was a good investigator. Also, falling back on this open-investigation nonsense is ridiculous. Has anyone even looked at the case in twenty years?"

Caleb sighed and folded his arms. "Honestly, I have no idea when the last time anyone looked at it was. I asked our records clerk to locate the file. It's been in our dead-case file since before I even joined the force. She sent me an email earlier that it's waiting for me. I'll call down there and tell her it's okay for you to sign out a copy."

Tucker thanked him, then turned and stopped at the door before walking out. "One more thing. How do I get to the records room?"

Caleb gave him directions and he hurried down the hall and down a flight of stairs to the lower level. This police station was much smaller than the Dallas precincts he was used to, but he liked the small-town feel. Everyone he passed by nodded and greeted him. He'd been in town now for a few weeks, long enough for most people to know who he was. He was a Harmon and, even after his grandfather was gone, his arrival in town was noted.

Tucker hurried down the steps and met a silver-haired woman sitting behind a desk with a sign that read Records.

"Hello there, ma'am, I'm—"

"I know who you are, Tucker Harmon. I used to see you kids in church every week when you were a child living at your grandfather's ranch." She reached out her hand. "Mazie Rutherford."

He didn't recognize her, but who remembered adults who were friends with their parents? "It's good to see you, Mrs. Rutherford. My cousin said you had a dead file for me?"

She nodded. "He called down and told me you would be picking it up." She opened her desk drawer and pulled out a file. "Here you go."

He took the file she handed to him, confused. "This was a missing-persons case. This can't be all there is?"

"It's been twenty years. If there were any other files, they're long gone."

"How does an entire case file vanish?"

She stood and faced him. "I remember this case. I wasn't working here then but you couldn't help hearing about it. I remember there wasn't much evidence to process."

He'd been involved in police cases before and he knew there should be a lot more evidence than one small folder, but this was a small town and an old case. He shouldn't be that surprised, yet he was.

The fact that Caleb had never even heard of this case should have clued him in that very little had been done to work on it. Something like this should have scandalized the town. The fact that it had been buried instead had to have been at the wish of Chet Harmon.

He took the file, thanked her and walked out.

He drove to a local diner and camped out in a corner booth, ordering a burger and fries and munching on them as he thumbed through the file. There was a statement from the officer on scene detailing the initial call, then another summarizing the search for Tonya. The only witness statement was from Chet Harmon and it apparently had been taken as gospel since no other statements were included in the file. Had they interviewed other witnesses? He didn't even see a list of people who'd been on the ranch at the time she vanished except for the one provided by his grandfather.

He shook his head. It was no wonder this case had gone cold. There should have been at least dozens of witness interviews, Tonya's financial and phone records, and photographs of the crime scene, assuming they could find one. Had these things been lost in the ensuing years, or had they not been performed at all?

Perhaps he could talk to some of the officers that were on duty during that time. He would ask Caleb which ones were still around.

Why was he bothering? That thought wiggled around in his brain and it was the same questioning look he'd seen on Caleb's face. He was supposed to be on a break, not diving into another case with someone he didn't even know. Yet, he couldn't forget the terror on Ally's face as he'd rescued her in the field.

Someone had shot her, and until they discovered why, she needed all the help she could get.

Plus, something Hannah had said was still bugging him. She'd remembered that Tonya's daughter had been found hiding in the barn. Ally had failed to mention that. He pulled out his cell phone. He'd copied the number and address of where she lived that she'd given to Caleb. He drove by her house but she wasn't home. Then he remembered she was a teacher at the local middle school. He glanced at his watch and noticed it was nearly time for school to be out. If she'd felt well enough to go to work, she would be there. Maybe he could catch her there before she left.

If she had questions about her mother's disappearance, he wanted to help her find those answers. And, unfortunately, the case file she'd hoped to uncover wasn't going to be much help.

He drove to the middle school and parked. The parking lot had cleared out, but there were still a few vehicles in the lot. He walked inside and stopped by the office, asking about Ally's room. The secretary gave him a visitor's pass then directed him down her area.

He walked through the halls until he found her classroom. She was standing in front of the whiteboard writing something that looked like notes for the next day. The desks were empty and there were no students in the room or in the hallway.

He rapped on the door and she turned, her eyes widening when she saw him. The bandage on her shoulder was covered up by her sleeve, likely for her students' benefit.

"Tucker, what are you doing here?" She dropped her notebook and dry-erase marker onto the desk.

"I wanted to speak with you about your mom's case." He motioned toward her arm. "I guess you felt well enough to come to work."

She nodded. "The pain wasn't too bad this morning so I decided to come. I didn't want my students to worry about me."

That made sense and he was glad to see her wound wasn't worse. He held up the file in his hand. "I managed to get my hands on her case file from the police station."

Excitement flashed through her eyes but then she sighed and her brow creased. "I've been trying for months to get ahold of that file with no success and you managed to get it in one day."

He understood her frustration. "Well, I am a cop."

"And the cousin of the chief of police. I'm sure that had something to do with it, too."

He couldn't deny that fact. He also couldn't deny that it wasn't fair. She hadn't been given access to her own mother's case. That wasn't right. He didn't blame his cousin. Caleb had staff that handled requests like that and Tucker believed him when he'd said he'd had no idea about the case.

She walked up and held out her hand. "May I see it?"

He handed it to her. She placed it on the desk, opened it and began flipping through. Tucker slid into a student desk that was clearly too small for him and was tight and uncomfortable.

Frustration quickly flooded her face. "This is all?"

"It's everything the records clerk found. I questioned it myself."

She picked up the paper with Chet's statement and read through it. "I don't understand. Why wasn't more done? My mother was missing. Shouldn't there be more to this case? This is what they've been keeping from me all this time?"

"It's possible the rest of the files have been moved or lost over the years. That's not uncommon in cold cases. Files and evidence go missing."

She sighed and slid into a chair beside him. "I thought by coming here, moving here, I was going to find answers, but I've only hit walls. It isn't fair."

"No, no, it's not fair. I can ask my cousin about searching the storage room for the old case boxes but that's kind of like looking for a needle in a haystack." Of course, she'd been searching a 5,000-acre ranch with no parameters. Talk about a futile search.

"Do you think they're there?"

"I have no reason to think they are. The lady in charge searched. We might be better off starting a new investigation from scratch."

"How do we do that?"

"We need to interview witnesses, find out who was at the ranch the day she vanished, maybe pull up old phone records if they still exist. What do you remember about your mom?"

She smiled. "She was very beautiful and I remember how she loved to laugh. We used to run in the fields and ride the horses. She loved that place."

"And the day she vanished? I heard they found you hiding in the barn."

Her smiled faded and she shook her head. "I've blocked that out. All I know from that time is that a ranch hand found me hiding and crying in one of the stable stalls. Apparently, I was hysterical and couldn't tell anyone what had happened. I don't even remember that much. I have a few memories of living and playing at the ranch, but my next clear memory is when I was already living with my aunt months later."

He rubbed his chin. Blocking out a memory wasn't uncommon after a trauma, but her lack of memory from that day was an obstacle he hadn't expected. When Hannah had told him she'd been there, he'd thought for sure those memories would have returned by now.

"I went through therapy for years but my memories never returned. My aunt encouraged me to journal, to try hypnotherapy. Nothing worked. I still have no memories of what happened that day. She never pressured me to try to remember, but after my aunt passed away, I discovered files about my mom's disappearance. Aunt Kay had been investigating the case all those years without telling me. She must have been so frustrated that I couldn't remember that day's events."

"Why wouldn't she tell you?"

"She always encouraged me to move on. I guess she didn't want me to get bogged down in trying to find answers. But she was doing the work all along while trying to convince me to let it go."

"So you picked up the case after she died?"

"I always had questions. I've always wanted answers and it was only my aunt's determination that I leave it alone that kept me from pursuing anything. I guess I could understand it while I was a child, but I'm an adult now. She should have clued me in to what she was doing."

"I agree. She shouldn't have left you in the dark."

"I'm sure she was only trying to protect me, but not knowing what happened to my mom has always plagued me. That's when I discovered how your grandfather had been sending my aunt money for years to take care of me. He paid for my college and purchased the house that we lived in. I don't know. It felt wrong. I me4an, I know she worked for him but why take care of me all those years unless he was somehow involved?"

That sounded odd to Tucker, too. He remembered Grandpa Chet as a stingy man. He hadn't been overly generous with his own family. He knew that he had never offered any kind of financial help to Tucker's mother after his dad's death. She'd struggled for years to raise him alone until marrying Tucker's stepfather. He'd long suspected she'd married him for the financial help but it had been a mistake. And he also knew that Luke had grown up only a few miles away from Harmon Ranch struggling to pay for basic necessities because his grandfather refused to offer his widowed daughter-in-law financial assistance. Grandpa Chet had had plenty of money, so that wasn't an issue.

It was a little disconcerting now to learn that he'd been offering assistance to a perfect stranger but not his own blood family.

Why wasn't he surprised?

Tucker rubbed his chin, pushing back lingering resentment toward Chet. "My dad died when I was a kid. My grandfather didn't lift a finger to help us. So, yes, I agree that his actions seemed suspicious. Do you know how long your mom worked at the ranch?"

"I don't know. I think it was years. Some of my first memories were from there. Your grandfather allowed her to bring me to work with her when I was little."

He didn't remember anyone there, but he had

a vague memory of a little girl playing in the hideout he'd built with his cousins. "Do you have a picture of your mother?"

She nodded, then went to get her phone and pulled up an image. "I took this from an old photograph I have of her."

Tucker looked at the image. She'd been a pretty woman with light-colored hair and a big smile. She wore a locket on a chain around her neck. "She was very pretty."

"Yes, she was. Thank you."

"I'd like to see everything you've collected, if you don't mind." The police file hadn't given them much information, so he was hoping she'd managed to collect some other interesting leads in her investigation.

She nodded. "I'm grateful for the help. Everything I have is at my house. You're welcome to come and look at it."

"Why don't I follow you home?"

She put her phone away but didn't immediately get up. "Why are you helping me, Tucker?"

It was a fair question and one he'd even asked himself. "My grandfather was a lot of things. A lot of not-nice things. That's how I remember him. That's how I've always thought of him. But I have a difficult time believing that he was capable of murder."

"So you're in this to prove his innocence."

"No. He's gone now, so it makes no difference to me what he did. But if he did help kill your mom or cover up what happened to her, that's not right. You deserve the truth and I want to help you find it. This won't be an official investigation. I don't work in Jessup, and I'm on leave from the PD in Dallas, but I know my way around an investigation, and at least you won't have to sneak around the ranch anymore."

She reached for his hand and draped hers over his. "Thank you."

"It's okay."

Tucker felt his hand tingling at the touch. Her skin was soft and he liked it, but he didn't want to go down that road. He wasn't ready for that kind of attachment with someone. He carried too much baggage. His role wasn't to be a husband and father. He'd come to terms with that a long time ago. His purpose was to help as many people as he could and he was happy to do so. After the fiasco in Dallas last month, he'd thought he needed time away, and he'd enjoyed his days on the ranch more than he'd expected. But he had a thing about power and influence being used to circumvent justice. He'd just had it used against him. It wasn't right that his family's wealth and position of power in town was preventing Ally from getting answers about her missing loved one.

* * *

He followed behind Ally as she drove to her house and parked in the garage. Once there, she motioned for him to come inside as she dropped her keys onto the island.

"All of my files are in the spare bedroom. I set it up as a mini office."

Tucker followed her down the hallway, where she opened a door. She had a bulletin board set up with her mother's photo as well as other information. He spotted his grandfather's photo on the board as well. He had no doubt the old man was involved in Tonya Fulton's disappearance. Now Tucker wanted to uncover whether Chet was the offender or behind the cover-up. Either way, his obstinance would be difficult to overcome even after his death. The damage to the case might already be irreversible.

She opened a box and handed him a manila envelope loaded with notes from the private investigator. "I spent years wondering and wanting to know what happened to my mother, but my aunt always encouraged me not to get obsessed with it. She would tell me that life goes on and we have to move on with it. It wasn't until after she died that I realized she'd been the one obsessed. She had all this information and she'd even hired a private investigator to help uncover the truth. He gave her a lot of information but no definite conclusions. He complained about the lack of assistance from the local police department."

Caleb would have been a child when Ally's mother went missing—however, last year, he was on the job. Had he turned away the investigator? He was the one person who'd remained close to their grandfather, having lived with him at the ranch since the age of twelve. Was he covering for their grandfather now? Tucker would find out. The Harmon name carried a lot of weight around town. He wouldn't say his grandfather had run the town, but he suspected whatever Chet Harmon had wanted from the town of Jessup, he would have gotten.

"What kind of information did he find?"

"He interviewed people who claimed my mother was having an affair with Chet Harmon. It was nothing definitive but that was the rumor at the time." He nodded. Hannah seemed to have confirmed that rumor for Tucker.

Ally had mentioned her aunt, but she hadn't mentioned anything about her father. Had he left them when he discovered the affair? Knowing his grandfather, he'd probably run the man off.

"Well, it's a fact that most people are killed by someone they know and the chances are great that a murdered woman was a victim of their spouse or boyfriend. What about your father? Where is he in all of this?"

She seemed a little shaken by his perfectly normal question. She lowered her head and picked at her nails. "I never knew my father. I don't even know his name. My mother was raped. Her attacker in that incident was never caught. I was the product of that assault. She never held it against me. She loved me. She used to say that God works all things for His purpose and I was the one shining light that came from that dark encounter."

Ouch. No wonder he'd hit a nerve. "I'm sorry."

"Learning my father's identity would also mean discovering the man who'd attacked my mother."

"Didn't you ever want to know?"

"I did. I even purchased one of those ancestry kits. It connected me with a family, but I wasn't able to track down who in that family could have been my father."

"Did you get a name?"

"Williams. I spoke with a woman who was determined to be a third or fourth cousin, but she couldn't identify any males in her extended family that might have been my father. Then again, she could have just been protecting them. How do you ask someone if anyone in their family might have fathered a child through rape?"

He could see how that might have been a sticky situation. He knew nothing about genealogy, although he'd heard about a lot of crimes being solved that way recently in the news. But nothing beat good ol' investigative work and that was what he could offer her.

"Where did the attack take place?"

"Here in Jessup. My mother was living here at the time. She'd been working at the ranch for several years when it happened."

So he had another police file to pull. If this woman had been assaulted, then gone missing a few years later, the two cases should have been combined or, at least, connected and the rapist considered as a suspect in her murder. It was possible her rapist could have returned to finish the job. "How old were you when she went missing?"

"I was eight years old."

So it seemed unlikely the two attackers were the same person, barring any additional information. However, the fact that both had happened at Harmon Ranch piqued his interest. It had always been his belief that few things happened at the ranch that his grandfather didn't know about. "Do you mind if I take a look at the ancestry report?" He was certain she'd already traced the possibility that Chet Harmon could be her father, but he'd like to verify it wasn't him for himself.

She nodded, then pulled it up on her laptop and printed him off a copy. "This is what I was sent by the company."

He would check it out on his own. If his grandfather had been Ally's father, his financial support of her made more sense. If he wasn't, then Tucker was still baffled about why he went to so much trouble to make certain she was cared for. If he had been having an affair with Tonya, had he had something to do with her disappearance, or was it just guilt that he hadn't been able to help her?

He gathered some files to skim through, eager to talk to his cousin about why this case hadn't gotten more attention.

He followed Ally into the kitchen. "Would you like something to drink before you go?" she asked. "I have iced tea."

"That sounds good."

For some reason, he wasn't quite ready to leave her. She'd had a difficult few days and he was anxious to help her find the answers she was seeking, but he couldn't deny that the lovely shape of her lips pulled him in. He wouldn't act on his attraction to her, however. He wasn't in a good place to be in a relationship and she certainly didn't need another Harmon in her life. His family had likely been involved in her mother's disappearance. He couldn't change that, but he could do whatever it took to help her bypass the gate his family name erected.

She opened the refrigerator door and removed a pitcher of iced tea, then poured some into two glasses. She handed one to him and kept the other.

He rattled the ice in the glass but didn't take a sip right away.

Caleb had asked him why he was so invested in this woman's plight and he hadn't had a good answer. He didn't want to believe that Grandpa Chet was involved in any of this, but it seemed unlikely he wasn't. Tucker was straddling a fence between clearing his family's name and proving that all his anger and rage toward Chet Harmon had been justified. He was learning more things about Chet that he didn't like, but the fact that he'd provided for Ally all those years baffled him, especially when he couldn't be bothered to care for his own grandchildren at the same time.

His next stop would be to talk with Caleb about the assault case files and ask him about the previous chief, who would have been in charge of both of Tonya Fulton's cases. If the man was still living, Tucker had a few questions he wanted to ask him.

* * *

Ally was grateful for Tucker's assistance. It was the first light in the dark investigation into her mother's disappearance. At least he could push through the brick wall that had been used to stop her from investigating.

After Tucker left, she made a quick run to the grocery store, then drove home and parked in her garage. She'd purchased this house only a few months after relocating to Jessup with the money she'd received from the sale of her aunt's house—the house that had been purchased for her with Chet Harmon's money.

She still shuddered about that.

It felt wrong to use it, but to not use it also seemed foolish. It wasn't like she could give back all the money. Plus, she wasn't one hundred percent sure that Chet Harmon had been involved in her mom's death. Without a proper investigation, she might never know.

It didn't make sense for Tucker to stick his neck out for her, yet he had. He'd gotten the file from the police station when she hadn't been able to. She was thankful for that, too, although it only confirmed to her that having money and influence in this town got things done.

She carried her groceries inside and set her keys on the island. After putting her items away, she poured herself another glass of iced tea, sipping it as she eyed the photo of her mother and aunt on the mantel. It was a favorite picture of hers. She traced her mother's face. How she wished she could remember her more. If only she hadn't blocked out everything from that day. She had to have locked it up inside.

A noise grabbed her and she spun around at the sound.

Someone was in the house.

She set down her glass, flipped on all the lights, then moved down the hall toward the bedrooms. She checked each one but found nothing. Had it just been in her mind?

She did her best to calm down. She rubbed her shoulder, obviously on edge. Being shot had a way of putting her on high alert. She had to be imagining something that wasn't there.

But someone had shot her. She hadn't imagined that. Her wound still ached and the bandage was itchy. Had she been targeted because she was finally onto something? Or had it simply been a nefarious group trespassing on the land, as Caleb believed? Tucker didn't seem to think so, or else he wouldn't have been so quick to step in and help her.

Unsure what to believe, she did her best to calm down. No one was inside so she must have been hearing things.

Ally slipped off her shoes then walked into

the kitchen to fix herself a sandwich. She should have eaten before she'd left and she might not have spent so much on groceries, but she hadn't and now her stomach grumbled for sustenance.

The butter knife seemed especially heavy in her hand and she felt groggy as she tried to spread mayo onto a piece of bread. She set it down, but sent it flying into the jar, causing it to tumble off the counter. She couldn't control her hands and she was suddenly so sleepy.

Something was wrong.

She reached for the glass of tea. It was the only thing she'd consumed since arriving home. She tried to grab for it and only succeeding in knocking it over.

She fell, too, hitting the floor. She couldn't move to reach for her cell phone. She couldn't move at all. The room began going black, but before darkness took her completely, the back door opened and two legs moved into her vision.

She tried to scream for help but no sound came.

As the intruder reached down to grab her, everything went black.

THREE

"You gave her the file?" Caleb let out a frustrated sigh. "That's police property, Tucker."

"No one has even looked at that file in over twenty years so what does it matter?"

"It matters because it's police property. You know better, Tucker. Get it back from her."

But he wasn't giving up so easily. "This lady has been denied answers about her mother's disappearance because our grandfather interfered with the investigation. That's not right, Caleb. And this police department has continued to hinder her search for answers. I want to help her. I think we owe it to her to investigate this."

Caleb leaned against his desk and crossed his arms. "Does that mean you're staying in town?"

He shrugged. "I have no set plans right now."

Caleb must have seen how serious he was about pursuing this. It wasn't right that his family's influence kept Ally from getting proper answers with regard to her mother's disappearance, even after all these years.

Caleb sighed then gave in. "I'll call down to Records and have them search. There has to be more to that case than simply that one file folder. I didn't know the last chief that well but I've only heard good things about him. I don't know why her mother's disappearance wasn't investigated more thoroughly. In fact, I don't know that it wasn't until we locate the remainder of those files."

Tucker had an idea why it might not have been. "If Chet was considered a suspect, he could have derailed the investigation, don't you think?"

"I don't want to believe that. I know he wasn't a nice guy, but a killer? I have a hard time believing he was that bad."

"Ally found evidence that he bought her aunt a house and paid for her school tuition."

Caleb turned to him, stunned. "Our grandfather?"

"Yep."

"Grandpa Chet was supporting her for her entire life?"

Tucker nodded. "I haven't seen the proof but that's what she claims she discovered after her aunt died. Why would he do that unless he was somehow involved in her mother's disappearance?"

"Why would he do it if he was involved? Either way, it inserts him into the case."

Caleb walked out of his office and Tucker followed him. As they were walking, he heard the dispatcher taking a call.

"We have a report of an intruder at 872 Oakdale Avenue."

The address was familiar. He recognized it as Ally's. He hurried over to the dispatcher.

"What was that call about?"

"A neighbor reported seeing someone lurking around the house and called it in."

He turned to Caleb. "That's Ally's address."

Caleb turned to the dispatcher. "Who's en route?"

"Jacobs and Withers are both responding."

"Let them know I'm on my way, too." They hurried out to Caleb's SUV. Tucker pulled out his cell phone as his cousin drove and dialed Ally's number, his gut clenching when she didn't pick up.

"She's not answering," he told Caleb, ending the call.

"I'm sure it's nothing. Nosy neighbors are notorious for overreacting. For all we know, it could have been a delivery driver or someone she knows."

Tucker knew he was trying to reassure him, yet his cousin pressed the accelerator even harder as they turned onto her street.

They arrived before the other responding officers, who pulled up in their cruisers as Tucker and Caleb were getting out.

"You both go around the back," Caleb called as he and Tucker rushed to the front door. The garage was down and the house appeared to be secured but he wasn't leaving without making certain.

Tucker reached the door and pounded on it. "Ally, it's Tucker. Are you home?" He heard no noises from inside. He glanced through the front window. No one appeared to be in the house and he saw no evidence of anything being out of place.

Had Caleb been right that the neighbor had overreacted?

He pulled out his phone again and dialed her number. It rang, but he also heard a ringing from inside the house. He glanced through the side window again and spotted it on the floor in the kitchen, lighting up.

"Her phone is on the kitchen floor but she's nowhere to be found." He ran to the garage to try to see if her car was inside. The door was down but there was a thin, high window on the side. He pulled himself up and peered inside—he could see the car, but he saw something else, too. Exhaust. The garage was filling with it and Ally was slumped over the steering wheel of the car.

He pounded on the window, but couldn't break it. It was made to prevent break-ins. They were going to have to get into the garage through the house.

He ran back to the front. "She's unconscious in the car inside the garage and it's filling with exhaust fumes. We have to get inside the house now." He picked up a planter from the front patio and busted through the front window then reached inside and unlocked the door. He pushed inside and rushed through the living room and kitchen to the door into the garage. He pulled it open and was greeted with exhaust fumes overwhelming him. He coughed, then took a deep breath of fresh air before hurrying into the garage. Caleb followed him and hit the button on the wall to raise the garage door.

Tucker opened the car door and switched off the engine. He noticed towels lining the bottom of the garage door, preventing the fumes from escaping. This was no accident. Someone had done this on purpose. He touched her cheek and she didn't respond, so he scooped her up into his arms and carried her out of the garage, placing her on the grass.

Caleb was on the phone calling for an ambulance as Tucker tried to revive Ally. She was pale and her lips were turning blue. That wasn't a good sign.

"Do you have any oxygen in your cruiser?" he asked Officer Withers.

"Yes, in the first-aid kit." He hurried to the cruiser, then returned with a small oxygen container.

Caleb ended his call. "The ambulance is on the way. How is she?"

"She's barely breathing." He placed the oxygen mask over her face. "Come on, Ally, breathe."

He was trained in life-saving procedures and if she didn't respond to the oxygen soon, he was going to have to start CPR. He checked her pulse. It was slow, but there. He had no idea how long she'd been inside the enclosed garage, or how much toxic air she'd inhaled.

He was thankful when he heard the sound of the ambulance and let the paramedics take over.

"What happened?" one of them asked.

"Carbon-monoxide poisoning. We found her inside the garage with the car running. It was full of fumes."

They worked on her for several minutes before loading her onto a gurney and into the ambulance. Her color was beginning to return and Tucker saw her pulse had increased. Good news. The oxygen was working.

Thank You, Lord.

He noticed a crowd forming in the neighbors' front yards. It wasn't uncommon to see onlookers when the police and an ambulance showed up. Caleb and both the officers who'd responded to the call were talking to the crowd, interviewing potential witnesses.

Tucker let them do that as the ambulance sped away with Ally inside. He walked back into the garage and pulled out his cell phone. The towels indicated someone had planned for this to happen. He was treating this as an attack against her life. He'd spoken to her just a few hours ago and seen no evidence of suicidal tendencies. She wanted answers for her mother's disappearance and he'd agreed to help her. She wasn't going to kill herself...not before she'd gotten those answers.

This had definitely been an attack against her.

He snapped pictures with his phone of the towels on the floor, the position of her car seat and the keys in the ignition. He hoped Caleb would have his crime-scene techs perform fingerprinting on the garage and doors. Someone was trying to stop her from uncovering what had happened to her mother.

He entered the house and walked through the kitchen. None of the entry points appeared to have been damaged or broken. So then how had the intruder gained access to her home? Had she let them inside? That indicated her attacker was someone she knew. And, if that was true, she should be able to identify them. Tucker needed to get to the hospital as soon as possible to question her.

He walked outside and found his cousin. "I don't see any evidence of a break-in, but you should have someone dust for prints."

"Are you sure this was an attack, Tucker? You haven't even talked to Ally. Maybe we're looking at something else entirely?"

He still didn't believe that, but they couldn't discount it until he'd spoken with Ally. "I don't think so, but I'm heading to the hospital. I'll find out. And, with no evidence of a break-in, she might be able to identify her attacker." At least, he was hoping so.

"We'll finish up here and secure the house, including the window you busted, and I'll post an officer to remain until you talk to her. If this was an attack, I'll have a team swing by and process the house."

That was a compromise Tucker could agree to.

Caleb handed over his keys. "Take my SUV.

I'll catch a ride back to the precinct with Withers."

Tucker took them, then climbed into Caleb's SUV and started the engine. He was anxious to talk to Ally, make sure she was okay and find out who had attacked her inside her own home.

Ally's head was pounding, but the oxygen was helping. She'd woken up inside the ambulance and the paramedic had recounted what had happened to her. He'd asked her questions about wanting to hurt herself and how long she'd had suicidal thoughts, then lectured her about the dangers of carbon-monoxide poisoning.

He thought she'd tried to kill herself.

She shook her head and pulled the oxygen mask from her face. "I didn't—"

The paramedic hushed her. "You need to keep this on."

She received the same treatment from the emergency-room doctor, so she kept quiet. They weren't listening to her, anyway, and the sooner she was out of this hospital, the sooner she could discover who had done this to her.

Her headache was easing with the oxygen as she lay on the hospital bed in a room in the ER and waited until she was recovered enough to leave. The door opened and Tucker entered.

Ally struggled to sit up in the bed.

"How are you feeling?" he asked.

She lowered the mask. "Tucker, I didn't do this. Someone drugged me."

"What do you mean?"

"The last thing I remember is being in my kitchen and then I got dizzy and groggy. I blacked out but not before I saw someone enter the house."

"Can you identify him?"

"No, I only saw his legs. The next thing I knew, I woke up in the ambulance."

His face showed skepticism as he pulled up a chair beside the bed. "How would someone have drugged you? There was no evidence of a break-in."

"I don't know how he got inside, but I felt dizzy after drinking the tea from my pitcher. Someone must have gotten inside the house. They drugged me, then placed me in the car in the garage. Someone was trying to kill me."

This time, she knew it wasn't an accident. She could have attributed being shot to a stray bullet but this incident couldn't be explained away so easily. Someone had come inside her house and attacked her.

His jaw clenched and he reached for her hand. "I won't let anything else happen to you."

She was glad to know he was on her side and

that he believed her. There was now no doubt in her mind that someone was trying to kill her.

Tucker remained with her while the doctor returned with her test results.

"It doesn't appear to be any lingering effects but your bloodwork did show evidence of a sedative."

She gave Tucker and I-told-you-so look. She hadn't taken any sedatives so that proved someone must have spiked her tea.

Tucker nodded. "I'll call Caleb and let him know."

The doctor released her after a few more hours of observation then Tucker drove her home.

Her garage door was down, but she still remembered what had happened... Well, she didn't remember it. That was the problem.

They climbed out and headed to her front door. The side window was boarded up and the door was locked. Tucker shrugged. "Sorry about that. I had to get inside. I'll make sure it's fixed."

"No, it's not a problem." She hadn't meant to make him feel guilty for doing whatever he had to do to save her life.

She stared at the door and realized she had no way to get inside. She tried the door handle. It was locked. "I don't have my keys with me.

We'll have to go inside through the garage." She walked around and looked at the keypad, noting that it was now covered in black dust— fingerprinting dust.

She keyed in the number and the door rumbled open. Her car was still inside and she touched it as she walked past. She pushed open the side door and stepped into her house.

"I didn't see any sign of forced entry so whoever got inside did so covertly. Did you hear anything?"

"I thought I heard something but then I didn't see or hear anyone. I thought I was imagining things. I didn't realize anything was happening until I felt groggy. I knew then that someone must have drugged my iced tea."

She noticed the tea pitcher on the counter beside the sink. It was now empty, but she was certain it had been half-full when she'd poured herself a glass earlier. "Did someone clean up in here?"

"No. They secured the scene, dusted for prints, then locked everything up. Why?"

"This pitcher wasn't empty. One of the last things I remembered was pouring myself a glass from it when I returned home. I didn't eat or drink anything else after that."

He picked up the tea pitcher and looked it

over. "It looks clean, but I'll take it to the lab and see if they can find traces of the drug used."

"This pitcher was nearly full. He must have dumped out the tea before he left. He probably just walked right out the front door."

He gave her a slight smile. "It's a good thing you have nosy neighbors. One of them made the call that brought us here to find you."

"I suppose I owe him or her a casserole or something. Is that enough of a thank-you for saving someone's life?" She looked up at him. She owed him, too. "I don't know how to say thank-you."

"You don't need to. I'm just thankful we got here in time."

She glanced around and shuddered, uncertain she would ever feel safe in this house again.

He must have noticed her hesitation. "Why don't I clear the house before I go?"

That did make her feel better. He checked each room then returned and gave her a smile. "No one is here and everything is locked up tight. You have my cell phone number. If anything happens, call me day or night, and I'll come. My cousin is also going to have a patrol car drive by. You'll be safe here tonight and I'll check on you in the morning."

She felt a little silly having Tucker watching over her this way but it did make her feel safer.

She cleaned up then got ready for bed. As she crawled into bed, she glanced at the picture of her mother. She wasn't going to let these attacks keep her from digging into her mother's case. If someone was trying to stop her from uncovering the truth about her mom, then they didn't know her that well. She wasn't giving up.

I'm going to find you, Mama.

With Tucker's help, she just might find the answers she'd been searching for.

FOUR

Tucker dropped off the tea pitcher to the police station and left it for the forensics team to examine. If Ally had indeed been drugged, as the blood test suggested, he hoped it would show up there, connecting the sedatives in her to the tea. However, the fact that the pitcher looked like it had been washed was troubling. Whoever had broken into her home had been there for a while. He'd taken his time to drug her, then place her inside her car in the garage to make people believe she'd died from suicide.

And he'd very nearly succeeded.

Tucker drove back to the ranch and parked Caleb's SUV in the driveway. He left the keys inside so Caleb could use the vehicle in the morning. He didn't want to wake him to give them to him and he knew the ranch was secure. They'd never had a car theft from the property that he was aware of.

He hurried upstairs to his bedroom. It was

the same room he'd occupied as a child, when he and his family would stay at the ranch. Until a few weeks ago, he hadn't been back since his father's death. He had good memories of the ranch, mostly playing with his cousins and spending time with his father and uncles, and even his grandfather. He recalled a time when Chet Harmon had been a kind and loving grandfather. Losing all four of his sons over the years had turned him bitter and he'd all but abandoned Tucker and his mom after his dad, Chet's third child, had died after being electrocuted while trying to clean up after a storm.

He peeled off his jacket, careful at the twinge in his shoulder from the gunshot wound he'd endured during his last mission with Dallas PD. Everything about that assignment had gone sideways, leaving Tucker injured and being forced to take some time off to heal and wait for the resolution of the situation. He'd finally decided to take his recovery time to deal with his inheritance. Caleb had convinced him that he couldn't put it off any longer.

He tossed aside his jacket, then got ready for bed. He'd thought a lot about those good childhood memories since deciding to return to Harmon Ranch. None of them, except for one vague memory he couldn't even be sure was her, involved a little girl or her mother.

Ally claimed she'd been a regular fixture at the ranch during the same time Tucker and his cousins had been here. He'd have to remember to ask Caleb if he remembered them.

Tomorrow, he would dig further into the disappearance and the attacks against Ally. Someone had tried to kill her more than once. The sooner they figured out who, the sooner they would have the answers they needed.

He couldn't explain his connection to Ally or his desire to help her, but he didn't like the idea that his grandfather might have had a hand in her mother's disappearance or, at the very least, had covered it up.

As he stretched out on the bed, his mind turned to his last mission. It had been a domestic-violence call, the most dangerous type of call a police officer could respond to. They'd known the assailant was armed and quickly set up a tactical area.

The situation had ended in Tucker shooting and killing the man who'd been terrorizing his estranged girlfriend. That hadn't bothered him. He didn't mind taking out bad guys when the situation called for it. What had really irked him was the response afterward. It turned out that the assailant's father was friends with the governor and Tucker's actions were scrutinized. He knew he'd acted appropriately and followed all the police procedures, but in a matter of a few hours of doing his job, Tucker had suddenly become the bad guy.

It wasn't right that someone with power could wield it against someone who'd only been doing his job, obviously choosing not to accept that their son had been the aggressor. Just like it wasn't right that Tonya Fulton could vanish without a trace and someone as powerful as his grandfather could cover it up, like she'd never mattered.

He couldn't do anything about his current situation. That would have to play out in Dallas PD politics, but he could do something to help Ally find the answers she sought.

He would do whatever he could to correct the mistakes his family had helped make.

Tucker was at Ally's door the next morning bright and early. He'd stopped and picked up coffee and doughnuts for them both.

She answered the door looking weary and he wondered if she'd managed to get any sleep. Dark circles beneath her eyes told him no. She was dressed in jeans and a T-shirt, and the shine in her eyes told him she was glad to see it was him.

"Did I wake you?"

She shook her head. "No, I've been up for

hours. I was just about to make some breakfast."

He held out the coffee and doughnuts. "Beat you to it."

She smiled then opened the door wider and motioned him inside. "I appreciate that."

She set them up at the table, grabbing some napkins and plates for the doughnuts. She bit into one, then gave a satisfied moan. "Delicious. Where did you get them?"

He noticed the photo albums opened on the coffee table, but didn't comment. She'd obviously spent more time looking through them. "I stopped at a gas station on Main Street for the coffee. They had them."

She nodded. "I know the place but I've never had their doughnuts. Usually, I'm in too much of a rush in the mornings to stop and get breakfast. I have to be at the school pretty early. Well, except for today. After what happened last night, I decided to take a personal day."

He could understand that. She'd had something very frightening happen to her. She needed time to process and recover from it. "I forgot that you've been in town way longer than I have. Guess that makes you the expert. I haven't lived here since my childhood and nothing looks the same as I remember. It's a completely new town for me to explore."

"I like Jessup," she admitted. "I came here to find answers about my mom and took the job at the middle school out of necessity, but I've come to really like the people and the community. Everyone has been very welcoming to me. I'd heard that most small towns are very hostile toward outsiders, so it's been a pleasant surprise."

"Yes, everyone in the community has been really nice since I came to town, but then again, everyone knows my cousins and knew my grandfather. It's like having everyone you meet already know everything there is to know about your life." It was a little unnerving and Tucker wasn't sure he appreciated it. These people might know who he was, but that didn't mean they knew him. He hadn't set foot in Jessup in nearly two decades.

She finished her coffee, then wiped her mouth with a napkin. "Thank you for that. I appreciate it."

"No problem. I wanted to check on you, anyway, and see how you were doing."

He could see she was putting on a brave face. "I'm better. I was able to get some sleep. I'm just so frustrated by all of this. I don't know what to do. I'm not sure what my next step should be. I was looking through the file you got from the police department. We have no crime scene, no DNA. Nothing to prove what happened to my mother."

Tucker reached across and took her hand. "We will figure this out. We don't always have DNA. Cases were solved long before DNA even became a thing."

"So what are we going to do?"

"We're going to do good old-fashioned investigative work. Assuming these attacks against you are connected to your digging into your mother's case, we'll focus on both aspects as much as we can. I've already dropped off the tea pitcher at the lab and the police dusted for fingerprints. We know the lady that called in to the police station saw someone breaking into your house. Maybe one of your other neighbors saw something, too, that might lead us to the perpetrator. We can start by questioning them."

He'd seen his cousin and the officers on the scene taking witness statements, but hadn't heard if their canvass had been fruitful.

He phoned his cousin while Ally went to change clothes and freshen up. "Hey, Caleb. Did anyone from the crowd at Ally's house last night report seeing anything suspicious?"

"Only the neighbor across the street. Doris Wheaton. She's the one who called in the intruder to the police station. Unfortunately, she didn't have much in the way of a description.

All she could say was that she saw someone snooping around the house then running away. It was too dark to get a description."

"Thanks, Caleb." Tucker entered her name in his phone. It wouldn't hurt to check back in with her today. Perhaps she'd remembered something else. Although he knew that the first witness statement was usually the most trusted. "Do you have a list of the people your team spoke with?"

"I do. Why?"

"I thought Ally and I would go back and re-interview them. Maybe we'll find someone who saw something but didn't bother to stick around and talk to the police."

"That's not a terrible idea. We did identify several houses that have security systems based on the neighbors' comments. We're still working to contact a few of them to find out if they have doorbell or security cameras and, if they do, if the cameras picked up the intruder."

"Send me the list. We'll check it out," Tucker told him as Ally reentered the living room. She'd put on some makeup and let down her hair from its ponytail. She looked strengthened and more confident, ready to take on the world.

He ended his call with Caleb and, moments later, received a text message with the list of homeowners Caleb had mentioned. It was a good place to start. "Ready?" he asked her.

She took a deep breath then nodded. "As ready as I'll ever be. I'm sure the neighborhood is itching to learn whether or not I lived."

"Have you met any of your neighbors before?"

"A few. I know Mrs. Wheaton across the street. We've chatted a few times about lawn care."

"The lady that called in to the police?"

"That was her? Of course, it was. She knows I live alone and she's sort of nosy."

"Nothing like a nosy neighbor to keep you safe."

He held the door open for her, then they walked across the street to the Wheaton residence. He knocked on the door and immediately heard a dog yapping inside. A minute later, the door opened and a tall, older woman stood there. She smiled when she spotted Ally.

"Oh, Ally, I was so worried about you when I saw the ambulance last night. Someone said you'd been hurt. I'm glad to see you're okay."

"I am, thanks to you." Ally gave her a quick hug and Tucker thought he saw tears in both their eyes.

"Did you catch the guy?" She directed the question toward Tucker. Either she'd seen him with the police at Ally's place last night, or else his presence oozed law enforcement.

"Not yet. You told the officers last night that you couldn't see his face. Is that correct?"

"Yes, that's right. It was dark and he was dressed all in black. I couldn't see his face."

"Does your home have any security cameras or one of those video doorbells?"

She shook her head. "No, I don't have anything like that. Some of the neighbors do, but I never have. My little Trixie—" she patted the dog's head "—lets me know if anyone comes in my yard. She's the best security alarm I have."

He couldn't argue with that. Dogs did make great security systems, although the yapping he heard earlier wasn't likely to dissuade a burglar from breaking in.

"Thank you for your assistance, Mrs. Wheaton. Please, if you don't mind, keep an eye out on the house."

"I will," she assured them both.

Tucker and Ally knocked on a few more doors in the neighborhood and spoke to several people. No one else had witnessed the intruder, but two neighbors offered footage of their home video cameras. Tucker thanked them and provided his email for them to send the footage.

They returned to Ally's house. Tucker pulled up the video footage on his cell phone and scrolled through it while Ally prepared them both a lunch of grilled-cheese sandwiches and soup.

"Find anything helpful?" she asked as she placed a bowl of soup on the table for him. The hopefulness in her voice only made his conclusions more painful.

"Nothing. Only one camera captured an image of the perpetrator and, like Mrs. Wheaton said, he's difficult to see, much less describe." He clicked off the image and slid his phone back into his pocket.

Her face showed disappointment as she pulled out the chair opposite him and sat down. She bit into her grilled cheese and munched on it before continuing. "So what do we do now?"

"If we can't find any clues as to who broke into your house and attacked you, we'll just have to turn our attention back to your mother's disappearance. I'm sure it's all related. Someone knows what happened to her and doesn't want you asking questions."

"I agree. But I've already done everything I can to find out and the police file didn't give us any new leads."

"I want to find out as much as I can about the police investigation back then. We can start interviewing people who worked the case. Caleb said the old chief of police was a good man, but

I'm wondering why he didn't do a more thorough investigation when your mom vanished."

"So we're going to talk to him?"

He shook his head and gave a grim look. "He died years ago, but maybe his widow remembers the case. Even though we don't like to bring our work home, cops sometimes talk about the cases that bother us. Let's hope he shared something with her."

If that didn't pan out, he would find out which officers from that time were still around and question them about the case as well. Someone in this town knew why this case had not been investigated properly. He was determined to find out why and get Ally the answers she deserved.

Tucker helped Ally clean up the dishes from lunch, then they walked outside to his pickup. He keyed the address into the GPS and followed the directions to the house. She realized then that they were both strangers here in Jessup. Two people from somewhere else digging into a twenty-year-old case. No wonder they were hitting a brick wall. Even his last name of Harmon wasn't opening the doors she'd expected.

He parked and they climbed out and walked to an older home with a big back porch and flowers growing in beds along the path. A windmill made of tin cans spun in the breeze and wind chimes whistled a sweet song. This was just the kind of house she'd imagined when she thought about small-town country living.

Tucker knocked and a petite, older woman with short graying hair and glasses answered the door. She smiled at them both. "Yes? Can I help you?"

Ally let Tucker take the lead. He was the professional investigator.

"Yes, ma'am, Mrs. Edwards. I'm Tucker Harmon and this is Ally Fulton."

She recognized the name right away. Of course, she did. "Harmon? You're one of Chet's grandsons?"

"Yes, that's right. We were hoping we could ask you a few questions about a case your husband worked on years ago."

She pushed open the screen door and welcomed them inside. "He didn't often talk to me about his work but I'll see if I can help you. Come on in. Would either of you like some sweet tea or lemonade?"

"Lemonade is fine," Tucker told her and Ally agreed.

"Fine with me, too, if it's not too much trouble."

"No trouble at all. I already made up a batch." She motioned them to sit at the table, then disappeared into the kitchen, returning a moment later with a pitcher of lemonade and three glasses.

She filled each and Ally took one from her, then sat down. "You have a beautiful house here," she commented.

Mrs. Edwards glanced around and Ally saw tears fill her eyes. "Yes, it's been my home now for the past forty years, but I'm selling the place and moving closer to Dallas to be nearer my daughter. She worries about me being out here all alone."

"I'm sorry to hear that. Family is important."

Mrs. Edwards smiled. "Yes, it is. But you didn't come here to talk about my family, did you now?" She slid into a chair and Tucker and Ally followed suit. "Which case are you investigating?"

"The disappearance of Tonya Fulton twenty years ago. She was a bookkeeper at Harmon Ranch."

She nodded. "I remember it well. Quite the scandal."

"Why is that?" Ally asked.

"Because of what happened to that poor little girl." She glanced at Ally and recognition popped into her expression. "You said your name was Ally Fulton. You were that little girl, weren't you?"

She nodded. "I was. I have no memory of that day. I was hoping someone else could tell me what happened but so far, I haven't been able to find the answers I'm seeking."

"My cousin Caleb gave us a look at the case file from Ally's mom's disappearance. There's quite a lot missing," Tucker explained.

"Oh, yes, that was one case that really troubled Stanley. He was convinced that something terrible had happened to that woman."

"It doesn't look like he did much investigating."

"Not officially, no. His hands were tied back then by the mayor, who was feeling pressure from Chet to close the case. He threatened to fire Stanley if he kept digging. Chet Harmon claimed the woman had simply left town. He provided travel receipts from a bus out of town and a motel where she supposedly stayed, but when Stanley tried to follow up, they led nowhere. He couldn't confirm she was the one on the bus or staying at the motel. Anyone who knew Tonya knew that she would never leave her daughter behind." She reached for Ally's hands. "You were the light of her life. She would never have abandoned you."

"You knew my mother?"

"Sure. We all went to church together. Back then, everyone knew everybody. I remember how she used to love to rock you in the church nursery and she would sing songs to you and the other children. She was a nice woman. No one who'd known her would ever believe she ran off, especially not my husband."

Tears welled up in Ally's eyes at the woman's reassurance. Ally had had her doubts throughout the years that her mother had cared for her, especially since a body had never been recovered. She'd dealt with the anger of thinking she'd been abandoned and that her mother had simply left her. However, those doubts had been long ago. Since growing up, she'd realized the truth. She knew her mother had loved her. She remembered the hugs and smiles and laughter they'd shared, and she knew in her heart she would never have left her. But hearing it from someone else—someone who'd known her personally—affected her, confirming her worst fears.

"Did no one question what happened to her?"

"Well, I'll tell you. Small towns tend to have a lot of rumors spreading like wildfire. My Stanley tried to sift through them, but he had to do so on the side. Paul Carlson was mayor back then and he was terribly afraid of Chet Harmon. He had ambitions for higher office and he knew he needed your grandfather's backing in order to get there."

Tucker's jaw clenched and his face flushed. Like her, he was probably bothered by the fact that his grandfather had managed to curtail an investigation. But why would he do that when her mother had been a faithful employee for years? Unless he'd been involved in her disappearance.

Tucker asked the question she was wondering about. "Why would Chet not want your husband to investigate? Did he have any idea?"

"If he did, he didn't say. He never believed Chet was involved. He believed Chet truly cared for Tonya, but he did manage to shut down the investigation. Without a body, there was little my husband could do. I know he checked her bank accounts and social security information and nothing was ever touched there. He continued monitoring them for years, even after he retired. He continued investigating as much as he was able. He was always haunted by what happened to that little girl." She looked at Ally. "What happened to you?"

"What do you mean?"

"They found you hiding in the barn. It was obvious that you were traumatized. Stanley was haunted by your cries until he died." Her eyes lit up. "You know what? In fact, I was cleaning out the storage shed a few weeks ago preparing for the move. I noticed a few of his boxes out there that held his old personal cases files. You might find something about your mother inside those."

Ally took in a sharp breath. Was it possible to find evidence hidden inside a shed after twenty years? What a break. But would it hold the information they needed to solve this disappearance and lead them to her mother's body?

"We'd love to look," Tucker said.

Mrs. Edwards nodded and stood, pointing out the window to a shed in the backyard. "It's unlocked. It used to be his office, where he'd spend his days after he retired working on old cases that he could never solve. I know he spent quite some time on that one."

"Thank you," Ally told her, giving her a hug.

The woman pressed her arms. "You're welcome. I hope you find what you're looking for." She stared at Ally and a warm smile spread across her face. She touched Ally's cheek. "You favor her, you know. She was so beautiful."

A wave of emotion flowed through Ally. She loved hearing about her mother. Aside from her aunt, she'd never known anyone who'd had firsthand knowledge of her. Ally hugged her again. "Thank you so much." Even if they didn't find out any information about what had happened to her mother, this visit had been worth it.

She followed Tucker out the back door and toward the shed. "Do you think we'll find anything in there?" She was encouraged to know that the former police chief had continued investigating her mother's case despite the political pressure. Hopefully, something in his research would lead them to answers.

He shrugged. "He wouldn't be the first cop to keep working a cold case that haunted him once he retired. Besides, we won't know until we look."

He pushed open the door. The shed smelled musty, but it was clean. Boxes were stacked along the walls and some had names on them. Tucker searched them until he found two that had *Fulton* scrawled across them. He pulled one down, then the other, and set them on an old workbench that had been cleaned off.

Ally stared at the unopened box as excitement bubbled through her. Did these boxes hold the answers she'd spent most of her life questioning?

Tucker loaded the boxes into his pickup. They'd agreed to take them back to her house to go through them. Skimming through them from inside an old shed wasn't the answer. He needed time to search them with a fine-tooth comb. Obviously, if the chief had ever found anything, he would have brought charges if he could, but had he discovered something that might be meaningful now that Grandpa Chet wasn't around to influence the case?

He double-checked that there weren't any other boxes with the name *Fulton* on them then thanked the chief's widow and they left, heading back to Ally's house.

Ally was shaking with nervous energy during the drive. He got it. After twenty years, they'd finally found something that might give her some answers. He was trying not to get his hopes up but he was excited, too. He couldn't wait to dig into those boxes and discover what leads or answers Stanley Edwards might have uncovered.

His stomach growled and he realized it had been hours since either one of them had eaten. "How about we stop for an early dinner first?" The earlier lunch had been several hours ago. They'd spent a good bit of time visiting with Mrs. Edwards and it was getting to be late afternoon.

She nodded. "Can we get it to go? I'm anxious to dig through these boxes."

That sounded like a plan to him.

He stopped at the diner in town and ordered sandwiches for them both. As they waited, he noticed a group of men sitting in a booth in the corner. He remembered a few of them from his time in town as a child. He knew men like this, who liked to gather for coffee and conversation every day. They usually knew the comings and goings of most things that happened in town. He wondered if any of them remembered Ally's mother's disappearance and what they would have to say about that.

His order arrived before he acted on that idea. Maybe he would ask them later if he needed to. He was still hopeful that the information from Police Chief Edwards's files was going to give them a good lead to Tonya's whereabouts and who might have killed her. And, assuming his grandfather covered up for them, who in his world did he care enough about to cover up for murder? Especially when he supposedly was so close to the victim?

Tucker took their food, then climbed back into his truck and they headed to Ally's. He pulled into the driveway, then they carried the boxes into her house. The room she'd designated as an office was small, so they stretched out in the kitchen/living room combo. She sat at the kitchen table while he sprawled out on the floor by the couch and opened one of the boxes.

Inside were various papers, piles of reports and notes taken by the former chief. Tucker even found some witness interviews inside.

Good. The chief had done his job and investigated this case. But why were they in his private file and not in the official police report? That baffled him. The pressure from the mayor—and, by proxy, Chet—to bury this case must have been great.

"Are you finding anything?" he asked Ally.

She shook her head. "Not much. Witness statements from people working on the ranch. I've written down a list of names. So far, I haven't seen anything that could give us any leads. Most of them claimed not to have seen anything. There are several mentions of finding me hiding in the barn and how upset I was."

He'd seen mentions of that, too, in the witness statements he'd read. It had been obvious to those questioned that something must have happened to Tonya because Ally had been hysterical with fear. Everyone in these witness statements seemed to agree that Tonya Fulton wouldn't leave of her own accord. But why had they accepted that narrative when Chet Harmon had floated it? Had they been protecting Chet, or their own jobs if they'd crossed him?

"We should still reinterview them. It's possible that they've remembered something in the years since."

"Why would they say so now instead of

back then, when they were first interviewed? Wouldn't their memory have been better then?"

"Sure, but sometimes people hold back. It's possible they were hiding something in their own lives that they didn't want the police to uncover—drugs, affairs, theft, something. After all these years, those things won't matter as much, so they might be more forthcoming. Also, loyalties change. Relationships end, giving people less reason to cover for someone else. People who were loyal to my grandfather might not have the same concerns now that he's dead. Our only choice is to reinterview everyone we know was at the ranch that day. Also, people talk. We just need to figure out who our killer has spoken to over the years."

"We should start with the staff at the ranch. I wrote down a list. If Chet was covering for someone, it would have to be someone close to him, don't you think?"

He did and that was the problem. He stared at the list of names she'd organized. He knew some of these people. It was unthinkable that someone he knew, someone that Tucker had known since childhood, might be a killer, but Ally was right. His grandfather had commanded loyalty from his employees and it seemed likely they might stay quiet to protect him. But, if he wasn't involved, was there someone in Chet's life that he would cover for? He didn't know, but logic was telling him the simplest answer had to be the truest. His Grandpa Chet had known and cared for Tonya Fulton. Had he killed her, too?

Ally rubbed her shoulder and the grimace on her face told him that this day had worn on her. It had been less than twenty-four hours since someone had attacked her and tried to kill her with toxic fumes. And only a day earlier, she'd been shot in the shoulder on his property.

Had it only been two days since he'd met her? It seemed like more. The hours they'd spent together had bonded them in a way he couldn't explain. He needed to prove to her that he wasn't like his grandfather, that he believed that people should find justice for their loved ones and not be run over by power and politics. That had always been important to him but, now, it seemed doubly important.

"Maybe we should call it a night and start bright and early tomorrow," he suggested.

For a moment, she looked as if she might argue, but then she gave in. "That might be a good idea. I am pretty tired."

"Is your shoulder wound bothering you?"

She did her best to downplay it. "A little, and my head aches. I think I need some Tylenol and a good night's sleep."

"I understand. If you don't take it easy, that shoulder could get stiff." She looked at him and he grinned and pulled up his sleeve to show a similar wound.

She reached out and touched the scarred skin over his wound. Her touch sent sparks racing through him and he shuddered. "I'm sorry," she said, jerking her hand away.

"It's okay. It just tickled a bit."

"How did it happen?"

"On the job. My team and I responded to a domestic-violence call. A hothead with a gun was threatening his girlfriend. I tried to defuse the situation, but it didn't work."

"He shot you? Did you save the woman?"

He shook his head and her expression fell. "I'm sorry."

"It gets worse, if you can believe it. This particular bad guy had a father who played golf with the governor. He didn't take too kindly to me shooting his only son. Technically, I'm on medical leave, but…"

"They're blaming you."

"Yes, they are. Big-city politics at its finest."

She sighed. "I don't think I like big-or small-city politics. Why can't people just do their jobs?"

"I feel the same way, but I guess that's not

the world we live in, is it? We have to play the game."

"I don't care for games."

She touched his arm in what he was sure was meant as a gesture of solidarity. However, at her touch, all the air seemed to leave the room and he was hyperaware of the heavy beat of his pulse.

"I should go." His voice cracked when he spoke and he quickly cleared his throat.

She must have felt that connection, too, because she lowered her head and nodded, clearly hurt by his abrupt pulling away. It was better for them both in the end.

"Why don't you come by the ranch tomorrow after school? I'll talk with Ed about getting a list of people who worked there during that time. We can compare it to the list of witness statements we have. Maybe we'll find someone who's never been interviewed."

"I'm not working tomorrow. I have a doctor's appointment scheduled for ten a.m. to follow up on my arm, so I took the whole day off."

He stared at the shoulder where she'd been shot. She didn't complain about the pain much, but he saw it still ached. He knew from experience it would for a while. "Great, then. Why don't you come by the ranch in the morning?

We can work out a game plan, then start interviewing after your appointment."

"Okay, I will." She nodded, but didn't lock eyes with him as she walked him to the front door.

Tucker hurried from her house, yet he still waited at the door until he heard the click of the lock before climbing into his pickup and starting the engine. He took a moment to catch his breath. He couldn't deny the attraction to her he felt. It had taken nearly everything in his being to leave her when he enjoyed her smile and her determination and the smell of her shampoo.

The Harmon family had already hurt her so much. He didn't need to add to her pain.

FIVE

Tucker awoke early and took his coffee on the side porch as dawn broke. He loved the view of the ranch against the morning light and the scents of grass and livestock.

He hated to admit it, but he was enjoying his time at Harmon Ranch. He'd fought returning here for so long, worried about what coming back here would mean. Would accepting his grandfather's inheritance mean that he'd forgiven him? Because that was something he'd been unsure he could do. Was still unsure he could do.

He bore the scars of the beatings his stepfather had given him during his childhood. He would live with those for the rest of his life and he still blamed his grandfather for leaving him in that situation. If he'd only reached out, if he'd never turned away from them in the first place, Tucker's life might have been different.

So he'd put off coming back here and facing those memories he'd tried so hard to hold back.

He finished his coffee then slipped on his cowboy hat and headed down to the barn to talk to Ed. He'd been working at the ranch since before Tucker was born and had been manager for as long as Tucker could remember. He would know who had been working at Harmon Ranch when Ally's mom vanished and, as manager, he might still have a record of employees from that time.

He spotted several of the ranch hands leading the horses into the corral and stopped to stroke one. The ranch had an amazing stable of horses. Horseback riding had been one of his favorite activities when he'd been a kid, but he hadn't done much riding since then until he'd returned to Jessup. Now, he'd been on one nearly every day and felt more alive and freer than he had in a long time. Maybe he should just quit his job at Dallas PD and take up ranching instead.

"Good morning, Tucker." Ed greeted him with a big grin. Ever since returning to the ranch, Ed and Hannah had both acted like it hadn't been twenty years since they'd seen him. They probably both still saw him as that scrawny ten-year-old kid he'd been. He couldn't deny it felt good to know someone still cared enough to try to look out for him.

"Morning, Ed."

"What's got you up and around so early? I thought you were on vacation."

"I've always been an early riser."

"You thinking about taking one of the horses out? I can have one saddled up for you."

"No, not today. Actually, I wanted to speak to you. Do you remember a woman who used to work here twenty years ago named Tonya Fulton?"

He rubbed his chin then nodded. "Sure, I remember her. I heard she ran off with some boyfriend, right?"

That was one of the rumors floating around, but Tucker was convinced she didn't leave voluntarily. "Actually, I'm helping her daughter figure out what happened to her. We don't believe she left on her own, but that something happened to her right here on the ranch."

Ed thought for a moment. "I have a hard time believing that. From what I recall, she didn't have any enemies."

"How well did you know her?"

"Not very well. She worked for your grandfather but she and I didn't converse much."

"Do you happen to remember anyone who was working at the ranch during the time Tonya disappeared who you thought might have had something to do with it? Or was acting oddly at the time?"

"Can't say I do. Like a lot of folks, I assumed she'd run off. She was a pretty thing and probably had lots of boyfriends."

"Any specific boyfriend?"

"No. I didn't know her well enough to have that kind of information. That's just my opinion. She wouldn't be the first woman to run off with a fellow and leave her kid behind."

That might be true. He'd known many women who'd chosen their boyfriends or spouse over their kids. He'd even once worked a case where a single mother murdered her toddler because her boyfriend didn't want children. That level of selfishness sickened him.

But Ed's perspective of Tonya Fulton didn't gel with the kind of mother her sister, or even Mrs. Edwards, had described. And, by his own admission, Ed hadn't known Tonya as well as they had.

"We'd like to speak to anyone who was working at the ranch back then. I was hoping maybe you still had some employment records." Most places had moved to digital files twenty years ago and he was hoping Harmon Ranch hadn't been behind the times. Keeping up with digital files was much easier than paper ones that could have been tossed out years ago.

"I'm not sure I do," Ed told him. "That's from a long time ago. Besides, I'm only in charge of paying the ranch hands and barn expenses. I have to turn in everything to an accountant every quarter."

That might be good for them. An accounting firm would be more likely to have digitized. "Bill Collins, right? I can try to contact him. Maybe he'll have those records."

"I'll tell you what, though," Ed continued. "Before you waste your time going to see him, I have a pretty good memory. I can probably give you a list of everyone who was working here at that time."

"That would be great, Ed. Thanks."

He nodded. "I'll work on that today and get it to you by morning."

"Today would be better if possible. I appreciate it."

He heard a car approaching and turned to see Ally's vehicle heading up the drive, kicking up dust behind it from the dirt road.

He hurried out to meet her as she pulled in and parked beside the barn. He opened the door for her as she shut off the engine. "You made it."

"I'm not too early, am I?"

He soaked in the whiff of her scent that floated through the air as she got out and greeted him. "Not at all. I'm glad you're here." He led her toward the barn, to where Ed was still standing. "I'd like you meet someone. Ed Lance, this is Ally Fulton. She's Tonya Fulton's daughter."

Ally reached for his hand and, after a moment's hesitation, Ed shook it.

"Are you okay?" Tucker asked him.

He nodded, but could hardly take his eyes off Ally. "Maybe it's because we were just talking about her, but I'd have sworn that was your mother heading toward me. You look just like her."

A smile spread across her face. "You knew my mother?"

He seemed to snap out of his reverie. "Not well, but I did know her. I knew you, too. In fact, you couldn't have been more than this tall when you started hanging around the stalls wanting to help groom the horses." He held his hand up to his knees.

She pushed a stray hair away from her face and her eyes widened. "I think I remember that. I think I remember you, too. You gave me carrots to feed to the horses."

He nodded. "I did." Emotion seemed to overtake him and Tucker assumed he was also reliving the past. "It's good to see you again, child."

"You, too."

"Let me know when you have that list ready," Tucker reminded Ed as he took Ally's elbow and led her toward the house.

"I'll go work on it now."

Tucker stayed close to Ally as they walked, enjoying how energized she looked this morning. "You look good. How'd you sleep?"

"I actually got a good night's rest. I'm feeling stronger today."

"I'm glad to hear it. I asked Ed for that list we talked about. He seems to think he can remember everyone who was working here at the time your mom vanished, but I can also check with the accountant in town. I'm hoping he might still have payroll records."

"Ed said he knew my mom. What does he think happened to her?"

Tucker didn't want to upset her, but it wouldn't be the first unfounded rumor she'd heard about her mom. "He also thought she ran off, but as he admitted himself, he wasn't close to her. He was just listening to the rumor mill."

She stopped walking and stared up at him. "I hate that people have all of these ideas about what she did. That they think terrible things about her."

"What people believe doesn't matter. We're going to find out the truth and put all these rumors to rest. I don't believe she ran off, Ally. The people who knew her best—your aunt, even Mrs. Edwards, who knew her from church—don't believe she would ever leave you. Neither do I. Besides, according to Police Chief Edwards's research, her bank accounts and social security number have never been used. And most people who go missing on their own usually come back for the big life events or reach out to family after a few years."

Something clouded her eyes. "I always looked out for her, you know. At graduation, at Aunt Kay's funeral, there was always an empty seat where she should have been. I also held out that little bit of hope that she would show up and celebrate with me. She never did." Her chin quivered and, for a moment, he thought she might start to cry.

He put his arm around her and held her in case she did. "I have big shoulders, Ally. Feel free to use one whenever you need it."

She stared up at him, her eyes searching his for something. Finally, she smiled. "I might take you up on that."

"Please do." But for now, he wanted to see her smile again. "Are you hungry? Have you had breakfast?"

"Yes, I had some toast and coffee before I came over."

"That's not breakfast. What you need is a good, hearty, Texas breakfast. I'm cooking." He held out his hand for her to take. "What do you say?"

She glanced at the house, then reached out and placed her hand inside his.

Her trust in him warmed his heart, spurring him on to help her in her quest.

But first, breakfast.

Ally stopped abruptly as they reached the farmhouse. She stared up at it. Her heart had been hammering nonstop since the moment she'd driven under the sign post that read *Harmon Ranch*. She was here, back where it had all started. Back where she and her mother had lived for the first eight years of her life. Back to where her mother had likely lost her life.

They'd lived in a private room in the back and seeing this farmhouse today made her lose her breath for a moment at the swell of emotions rushing back to her. She recalled the garden at the side of the house, where she'd helped pick vegetables, and running around her mother's little office as she used her calculator to crunch numbers.

She put her hand on her chest to push back

the emotion threatening to overwhelm her. She hadn't expected this. Of course, it wasn't her first time back on Harmon Ranch. She'd spent months searching the acreage without being seen. But this was the first time she'd been back to the house and the memories of where she'd once lived and played were rushing back to her.

"Everything okay?" Tucker asked. He didn't push her to plow forward and she appreciated that. He seemed to recognize that she needed a moment to process it all.

"When I used to think about Harmon Ranch, it was this abstract place in my mind that I couldn't really see. I don't think I remembered anything about living here until just now, when I saw the house. I remember being here, Tucker. Playing on those steps. Helping Ed brush the horses' manes, picking carrots in the garden."

He watched her closely. "What about…?"

She understood his question. Memories were flooding her, but still nothing about the day her mother had gone missing. That day was still a dark cloud she couldn't penetrate. "No. I still don't remember what happened to her."

He nodded and squeezed her hand reassuringly. "Maybe it'll come."

Or maybe it was a blessing that it hadn't. She'd heard that before. Aunt Kay used to tell her that she was better off not remembering the trauma of that terrible day. Perhaps she was, but if she could remember, she might be able to identify who'd hurt her mother and what he'd done with her.

Tucker gently pulled on her hand, urging her on. "Ready to go inside to get that breakfast? I make a killer French toast. Eggs. Bacon. Maple syrup. What do you say?"

Her stomach growled in response and they both laughed.

"I'll take that as a yes." He tugged at her hand again. "Come on, Ally. Everything will be all right. You'll see."

How had she come to trust this man so much? She still didn't understand it, but she did trust him.

She followed him inside the house and into the kitchen, where he led her to the table and pushed her into a seat. He grabbed a frying pan and set it on the stove, then opened the refrigerator and began pulling stuff out.

A woman entered the kitchen. "What's going on?" she asked Tucker.

"I'm making French toast, Hannah. Would you like some?"

She looked like she wanted to protest for a moment, but then smiled. "I would love some French toast. Sure you don't need some help?"

"Nope, I've got it," he said before making introductions. "Hannah, this is Ally Fulton. Ally, this is Hannah Murphy. She's lived and worked at Harmon Ranch forever."

Hannah leaned over and shook Ally's hand. "Not technically forever, but long enough that seems like it," she said, chuckling.

"It's nice to meet you, Hannah." Something about the woman's smile was familiar and she was sure she'd known her when she'd lived here as a child.

Hannah seemed to remember her, too. "*Fulton?* As in Tonya Fulton's daughter?" She glanced at Tucker, who gave her a nod.

"That's the one."

She turned back to Ally. "Tucker said you were back in town and looking for answers about what happened to your mom."

"Yes, I'm thankful he's helping me try to figure it all out. You knew her, didn't you?"

Hannah nodded. "Yes, I did. I guess I knew you, too, didn't I?" She suddenly laughed. "Oh, boy! Talk about making me feel old. It's bad enough you, Tucker, and your cousins have grown up so quickly. Now, here sits the little girl who used to help me fold laundry and work in the garden and help me bake."

Suddenly, the aroma of food cooking caused the memory floodgates to open again. All the things she'd remembered doing before, and now she remembered the woman who'd been with her. Hannah.

"I used to watch you in the afternoons after you'd gotten out of school while your mom was still working. You were always a good helper and a sweetheart."

"Do you think I could see the room where we stayed?"

Hannah glanced at Tucker, then back at Ally, and nodded. "Of course. We'll be right back, Tucker."

After getting up the courage to ask, she suddenly wasn't so certain she wanted to see it. But Tucker nodded, urging her on. "Go ahead. This might be good for you."

The way memories were pounding her, she wasn't so sure. But she stood and followed Hannah to the back of the house.

Hannah pushed open a door that held a double bed, a simple dresser and chest of drawers. Ally stepped inside. The furniture wasn't familiar and, for all she knew, was completely different from what she'd had with her mother. Nothing about this room stood out to her until she walked to the window and stared out at the view of the pasture. She took in a breath. She remembered running through that grass, laughing and singing, chasing after her mom.

"I'll take you to where her office was, too,"

Hannah said, and Ally followed her again down another long hallway. Hannah pushed open the door. "It's my sewing room now, but this is where your mom spent her days. After she vanished, Chet never hired anyone else. He sent everything to the accountant to handle instead. I don't think he ever got over losing her."

This room didn't spark any memories for her, either, but she supposed it might be because her mother's stuff was long gone from it. Her desk had been replaced with a sewing machine and craft table, and her photographs and papers were probably packed away somewhere or had been disposed of, at least the ones Ally and her aunt hadn't gotten.

"Thank you for showing me this, Hannah. It's helping to bring back some memories for me that I didn't previously have."

"I'm glad it's helpful." She pulled Ally into a hug and seemed on the verge of tears herself. "Now, let's go have some of that food Tucker insisted on cooking himself. I swear that man hasn't let me do anything for him since the moment he stepped foot back on the ranch."

Ally knew taking care of things was Hannah's job, but she could also see how much it meant to her. She'd been caring for the people of Harmon Ranch for so long that they had become her family.

Ally might have been a part of that, too, had her mother lived.

Whoever had taken her mom from her had also robbed her of that life and family.

Plates of French toast and scrambled eggs greeted both her and Hannah when they returned to the kitchen. She dug in and it tasted as good as it smelled. Tucker passed her the syrup and she spread it over her plate, spilling some on her shirt.

"Oh, no. I've made a mess."

Tucker handed her a napkin. "It doesn't look too bad."

"Still, after I finish this delicious breakfast, I think I'll head home and change before my doctor's appointment. I don't want to be a mess all day." She didn't know exactly what Tucker had planned for them to do later today, but she would feel more confident in a clean shirt.

"That sounds good. I want to check on some things with my cousin, then come up with a game plan for us. In fact, let's have another look at that ancestry report. Maybe I should just come with you to your house."

"That's not necessary. I can bring it back here. Plus, my car is already here and I have that doctor's appointment. Hopefully, it'll only take me about an hour or so depending on how busy he is."

"Okay, if you're sure."

"I am."

They all finished eating and Tucker cleared the plates.

"Just set those in the sink," Hannah told him. "I'll take care of them."

"No, I'll do them. I don't mind."

Ally stood. "I'll help, too."

"That's really not necessary," he insisted. "Why don't I walk you back down to your car, then I'll return and finish these. And, Hannah, don't you touch them."

Ally stifled a grin, wondering which one of them would win that battle of wills.

Tucker walked her to her car, which was down by the barn, and she climbed inside. "I won't be long," she told him.

He nodded. "I'll be waiting."

He headed back toward the house as she started her car, but before she could turn around, she spotted the stalls inside the big, red barn. The same stalls she'd been found hiding in the day her mom had disappeared.

Seeing the house and the view from her old bedroom, and even Hannah, had brought back a slew of memories from her childhood—memories she'd previously repressed. Maybe going back to the place she'd cowered in could jumpstart her mind to that terrible day.

She didn't want to relive it, but she needed to.

She glanced toward the farmhouse. Tucker had already disappeared up the path and was out of sight. He wouldn't think it was a good idea, but she had to do it. She shut off the engine and got out of the car.

She pushed open the barn door and stepped inside. She scanned the stalls. This was the place where she'd been found twenty years ago, the place she'd hidden while something terrible had happened to her mother.

If only she could remember what it was.

She walked past the stalls of horses, who mostly ignored her. The familiar aromas of the barn returned to her. She'd spent her days playing here as a child. Today, she'd been flooded with good memories of those days before the incident, before her mother had gone missing. She hadn't been near a barn or a horse since the day she'd been found. Her aunt had come and taken her home while the police searched for her mother. They'd never found her. Never found any indication of what had happened to her at all. Tonya Fulton had simply vanished and the only person who could tell what had gone on—Ally—had been too traumatized to remember.

Her eyes watered. Even all these years later,

that day was a dark void. Her mother was still missing and Ally still had no idea why.

She walked into the stall where the ranch hands had discovered her hiding and crying. She still didn't actually remember the events of that day, but she'd heard them told many times. The men who'd found her had brought her to the main house and the paramedics had been called. They'd searched for her mother only to discover she was nowhere to be found.

Ally had tried so many times to access the memories from that day through the years with no recall, but this was the first time she'd returned to the scene where it had happened.

She shut her eyes and tried to close her mind to everything except that day. The smells of hay and manure tickled her nose. The horses' neighing sparked flashes of memories skipping through her mind, but nothing stuck. She couldn't grab hold of any of them and couldn't even be sure they were the memories she was searching for.

Frustration filled her. Why couldn't she access the ones she really needed to?

Suddenly, something hit her from behind. Pain radiated through her head and she struggled to stand. Hands on her back shoved her into a stall. The sound of gunfire ignited a rush of activity inside the stalls. Spooked, the horses began jumping and kicking.

Ally screamed and raised her arms as horse hoofs came flying at her head.

SIX

"Ally!"

Footsteps ran toward her as she cowered in the corner. Big hands grabbed her and pulled her over the top of the stall. She was still trembling with fear as Tucker took her into his arms.

"Are you okay?" He quickly checked her over, then pulled her against him again.

She spotted two other men doing their best to get the horses under control and calm them down as she pressed herself against Tucker's safe embrace.

She'd nearly been killed and this had been no accident.

Tucker guided her from the barn and into the open fresh air. "Ally, what happened? What were you doing in there?"

"I—I was checking out the stall where they found me. I was hoping a memory would come back to me, but someone hit me, Tucker. I was hit from behind and shoved into the stall, then I heard a gunshot that made the horses go crazy."

His face tensed. "Someone did this to you on purpose? Did you see who?"

She shook her head. "No, I never got a look at the person. Whoever it was hit me from behind."

He rubbed the back of his neck and paced in front of her. "I was back at the house when I heard what sounded like a gunshot. I wasn't certain so I came to check it out." He turned to the two ranch hands dealing with the horses. "Did either of you see anyone?"

They both shook their heads. "We heard shots and came running but didn't see anyone leaving the barn," the older one explained.

So someone had been able to attack Ally, fire off a weapon and get out without anyone seeing. It didn't make sense. He turned back to Ally. "I didn't expect this. I'm sorry."

She was still trembling with fear, but he didn't owe her any explanations. "You have nothing to be sorry for, Tucker. This isn't your fault." She was the one who'd chosen to go inside and try to recover her memories. She'd just never expected to be attacked while doing so.

"I should have been more careful. You've been a target previously. I thought you'd be safe here at the ranch."

My mother hadn't been.

She didn't say that, but saw the look on Tucker's face that suggested he'd thought the same thing.

Her hands were still shaking, and suddenly she wanted to flee from this place. It felt unsafe just being here. This had been no accident. The person targeting her—and likely the person responsible for her mother's death—was here today at Harmon Ranch.

"I want to go home," she said, running to her car.

Tucker followed her, but held her door as she climbed into the driver's seat. "Are you sure you're okay to drive? Why don't I take you?"

As much as she felt safe with him, she didn't want to wait. She needed to leave this place. Now.

"I'll be fine," she assured him as she dug for her keys, then struggled to start the car with shaking hands.

He closed the door but leaned in through the window. "Get home and lock the door. Call me once you're there so I know you're safe. I'll come to your house once I figure out what happened here. If whoever did this to you is still on the property, I want to find him."

She nodded her agreement, then put the car into Drive and took off as he moved away.

The sooner she was away from Harmon Ranch, the safer she would feel.

Tucker watched the dust kick up after Ally's car as it sped away.

Anger boiled through him at the thought that someone on the ranch had attacked her. It was bad enough her mother was missing. Now, someone had tried to kill her here, too. Even with Tonya's disappearance, he'd never considered that Harmon Ranch wasn't safe. Although, she had been shot while out searching the property, he'd convinced himself that had been an anomaly. Was it possible that whoever had killed Tonya still worked and lived here?

He scanned the barn and corral area. The two men still working to calm the horses were too young to have been involved in Tonya's death. But someone had attacked Ally and what other reason would they have had except to stop her from trying to figure out what had happened to her mother? It was just too coincidental that this attack wasn't related to the other ones.

He marched to the side of the barn and found Ed, who was dealing with a delivery of feed being unloaded. The delivery driver looked to be fortyish, but the young guy unloading bags was in his early twenties at most.

Ed quickly signed a computer tablet, then handed it back to the delivery driver. The driver acknowledged Tucker with a nod, then headed back to his truck to help the younger guy finish unloading.

"How is your friend?" Ed asked Tucker. "She wasn't hurt, was she?"

"No, just shaken up."

"That's a blessing. Those two horses have been a bit jumpy for a few days now. I've had the vet out here looking at them to see if something is wrong. I can't imagine they would react like that to seeing someone, though."

"Ally said someone fired a gun and that's what spooked them."

Ed thought for a moment. "That would do it. I didn't hear gunfire, but a couple of the young fellas thought they heard something. They were going to check when they ran into you."

"I heard it, too." He was a little surprised that Ed hadn't.

He was quick to explain. "I was in my office at the time. Had the radio playing. Plus, I'm not getting any younger, you know. I don't hear as well as I used to."

Tucker wanted to believe that explanation, but as far as he could tell, there were only a few men on the ranch today who would have been old enough to be involved in Tonya Fulton's disappearance. Ed was one of them and had already admitted to knowing her. But could he have gotten out of sight before Tucker and the ranch hands rushed into the barn? Tucker couldn't remember when or where Ed had first appeared. He'd been too focused on Ally to pay anyone else much attention. And Ed didn't move as quickly as he once did.

"Someone attacked Ally today, Ed. I want to know the name of every person who was here at the time."

Ed nodded. "Well, there were the ranch hands, of course."

"They're too young to be involved in this, but jot down their names for me just in case."

Ed pulled out a notebook and wrote their names on it. "There was also Dr. Wilson, the veterinarian who was here to see about the horses."

"The ones in the stall where Ally was attacked?" He hadn't seen anyone else inside the barn.

"No, I think he was out in the corral checking on another horse when she was attacked. He'd already vetted those two."

Tucker nodded. That made sense, but he would need to hear it from Dr. Wilson himself. "Where is he? I need to speak with him directly."

Ed glanced through the window. "His truck is gone. He must have already left the ranch."

That seemed suspicious. Tucker didn't know the vet, but a quick trip to his office for a conversation was in order. "Who else?"

"The delivery from the feed store. That's everyone except for Hannah in the house. Jeb, our mechanic, is in the hospital with a sick child and the trainers have gone out of town to an auction."

That wasn't a long list and he'd already decided the ranch hands couldn't be involved. He'd taken their names, though, to check out. It was always possible they'd been paid by someone to target Ally. Plus, he intended to find out everything he could about the delivery driver and his coworker.

It was a place to start.

And speaking of lists… "Do you have that list of names of people who worked here when Tonya Fulton went missing?" He'd promised to work on it for Tucker.

"Sure do. Come on into my office and I'll get it for you."

Tucker followed him to the other side of the barn, where Ed had his small office in an extension. He looked to be something of a pack rat, and had books, files and papers stacked up. Hanging on the wall were framed photographs taken in front of the barn of different groups of people. Tucker glanced at them.

"Every few years, we hold a barbeque and fun day for the employees and their families. Anyone who has a connection to Harmon Ranch is invited. We try to do a group photo each year. Everyone seems to enjoy it." His expression fell. "I don't suppose we'll have one this year."

"Is there a photograph from when Tonya and Ally lived here?"

"Sure." Ed scanned the frames until he found one. He pulled it off the wall. "Here is it." He pointed to a woman holding a little girl. "That's Tonya holding her daughter."

In the photo, Ally looked to be around five years old, so a few years before Tonya went missing.

Each photograph had the date emblazoned on the front, so Tucker searched for the one from twenty years ago. "I don't see one from the year Tonya went missing."

Ed searched, then shook his head. "Like I said, we didn't do one every year. Seems like we must have skipped that year."

That was too bad. It would have been nice to have a photograph of everyone who'd worked at the ranch at that time.

"Thanks for this, Ed."

He took the lists Ed had given him, then hurried to his pickup. He didn't want to leave Ally alone for long and she'd been a wreck when she'd left. He would feel better knowing that she was safe and sound.

She still seemed shaken when Tucker arrived at her house and Ally opened the door. Fear was obvious on her face until she saw it was him.

He wanted nothing more than to pull her into a hug, but he saw her hesitation and didn't want to spook her.

He closed the door and she padded back to the kitchen. The kettle was whistling that her water had finished boiling.

"Did you find him?"

He hated to disappoint her but he couldn't lie. "No, we didn't. There were only a certain number of people on the ranch and most of them were too young to have been involved in your mom's case, unless they'd been hired to target you. That's a lead I'll certainly explore. I also got a list of their names. I want to check out their backgrounds."

She sighed as she poured steaming water into her mug over a tea bag. "I'm not sure I can today, Tucker. After what happened at the ranch, I just feel like I want to stay inside and hide."

"That's understandable. You had a scare. You need time to adjust and deal with it." But he wasn't ready to leave her, either. "I know we had planned on conducting interviews, but we can stay here and perform background checks on everyone on this list. We don't have to go anywhere."

A few hours ago, she'd been smiling and laughing, enjoying the good memories returning to her. Now, she was frightened and she had good reason to be. He wanted to find out who was after her, but more than that, he wanted her to be safe.

"I do still need to go to my doctor's appointment."

"Do you want me to drive you?"

She reluctantly nodded and he was relieved when she did. He wasn't ready to leave her side.

He drove her to her doctor's appointment and waited until she'd been given the all-clear by the doctor who'd checked out her wound. It was good to hear that the wound was healing nicely and no infection had set in.

It seemed odd to him that it had only been a few days since their first meeting in the pasture because she'd become such an important part of his days.

They went through a drive-through to pick up lunch and ate it back at her house. Then, while she rested for a while, Tucker spent the afternoon gathering as much information as he could on each person on the lists Ed had given to Tucker. It wasn't easy without the access to the Dallas PD he usually had, but he did his best searching through online sites and social-media accounts. Nothing was standing out to him so he decided to check in with his cousin later to see if any had criminal records.

It was early evening before Ally finally relaxed enough to sit still and help him go through the lists. He couldn't blame her for being shaken by the event. They'd both assumed the ranch was safe. It hadn't occurred to him until today that whoever had harmed Tonya Fulton might still be working there.

"Thank you for staying with me today, Tucker. It means a lot."

"You've had a scare. It's understandable to be shaken by it. I just hope it doesn't make you want to stop digging into your mom's case."

She shook her head. "I'll confess the thought has crossed my mind. Especially today. A part of me wanted to pack up and head back to my hometown and forget any of this ever happened. I think I would be safe if I did."

He hated to admit it, but that was probably true. She wouldn't be safe unless she either gave up the investigation into her mom's disappearance or they found the person behind these attacks.

"But I can't do that," she continued. "I won't be bullied into giving up. Someone terrible is lurking out there and that person hurt my mother and has now targeted me. I can't let them get away with that."

He grinned, proud of her strength and determination. "I won't give up, either," he assured her. "And I promise I'll do my best to keep you safe."

"I know you will. I honestly don't know what I would do without you here with me."

He glanced at the photos on the fireplace mantel. Ally at her college graduation standing beside another woman. The same woman standing with Ally as they both smiled at the camera. And, at the end of the mantel, an old photograph of Tonya Fulton.

Tucker picked up one of the photos of Ally and another woman. "Is this your aunt?"

She smiled and nodded. "Aunt Kay. My mom's sister. She took me in and raised me after mom disappeared."

He replaced the photo. "She looks nice."

"She was wonderful. I didn't truly appreciate all she did for me until she was gone. I miss her very much."

"How did she die?"

"In a car accident two years ago. It was late at night and she ran off the road and slammed into a tree. The police said she was killed instantly."

"I'm sorry. After all you went through with your mother, that must have been difficult."

She nodded and looked so forlorn. He checked the urge to pull her into a hug. "She was all the family I had left. I have no one now." She replaced the photograph on the mantel. "That's why it was so easy for me to pick up and move to Jessup. I had no one tying me down. I sold the house, packed up everything and took a job here."

"You must have had friends."

"Sure. Friends from school and church, but once I went to college, we all sort of scattered. Everyone went about their own lives. People got married and started having babies. I jumped into teaching. But, you know, life gets in the way. Aunt Kay was the last link I had to where I grew up."

He felt bad for her. He knew what it was like to be alone in the world. "I have to confess, I know how that feels."

"How could you? You have family, your cousins?"

He rubbed the back of his neck. He didn't often share his dark past with others, but he felt compelled to do so with her. "Actually, until a few weeks ago, I'd hardly spoken to or seen any of my cousins in more than a decade. We haven't been close in a long time."

"What about your family?"

"No real family. I left home when I was sixteen, lied about my age to join the army, then joined the police force once I got out."

"What? Why so young?"

"My stepfather. He wasn't a nice guy. He was abusive to both me and Mom. He made my life a nightmare. I couldn't take it any longer and my mother refused to leave him so when I got old enough to start fighting back, it just made things worse. She wouldn't leave him so I left instead."

"Is she still with him?"

He shook his head and swallowed back bile that rose in his throat at the call he'd received five years ago. "No. She killed him, then herself." She'd finally found the courage to fight back against him, but she'd been too devastated to try to build a life without him. "She could have come to me. I would have helped her, but she didn't. She didn't even try."

She touched his arm, sending a thrill of electricity through him. He hadn't shared that much of his life with anyone else. In fact, it was the first time he'd ever even verbalized what had happened to anyone. He couldn't explain the desire to open up to her, but he was glad he had.

She stood close to him and wrapped her arms around him, pulling him close. "I'm so sorry, Tucker. That's terrible."

He basked in her sympathy and with sharing a part of himself with her. But reality set in and he soon moved away from her. They'd both experienced pain in their lives, but they didn't have the time to dwell on that if they wanted to uncover the secrets of her mother's disappearance. The only past he cared about now was the disappearance of Tonya Fuller and his Grandpa Chet's involvement in it. "We should get back to digging through these records."

Her eyes widened and hurt filled them as he put some distance between them. "Of course. I—I'm sorry. I crossed a boundary."

"No, you didn't." He was quick to reassure her. "It's just that I've never told anyone about that."

"Oh." Her face registered shock, then softened. "I'm honored you shared that with me."

"I don't know why I did. I never speak about my personal life."

"Never?"

He shook his head then turned away. "I've always strived to be a good person, to help people. I do what I can. I'm always willing to step up and do whatever is needed at church or among my friend group, but I—I don't often share about what I went through. I want to help people, not burden them with my baggage."

She nodded and bit her lip. "I understand that, but sometimes sharing the load is helpful. You're helping me find answers about my mom. The least I can do is listen to what you've been through."

"I appreciate that, Ally, but I would prefer to just try to focus on finding the answers you seek." He had to keep his emotions in check and focus on the work. He couldn't allow his judgment to be clouded by emotion. He was trained better than that.

But he didn't miss the color of hurt that flashed on her face before she covered it with an understanding smile.

He closed his laptop, then picked it up. "I think maybe I'll head over to the police station and ask my cousin if I can use the police network to check for any criminal backgrounds. That might speed things up." He went to the door, but stopped to turn to her, feeling the need to say something that would make his awkwardness better. "I'll bring breakfast by in the morning then we can go conduct some interviews."

"Tomorrow is Friday, Tucker. I have school

all day. I don't feel right taking another day off."

He'd forgotten. "I'll see you after school then and let you know if I find anything."

He headed out quickly, but paused long enough to hear her lock the door behind him before sprinting toward his truck. He opened the door and loaded the files inside, then climbed in.

He paused before he started the engine. He couldn't believe how he'd opened up to Ally about his past. He never did that. He preferred to keep his dark past locked away so he didn't have to dwell on it. It was too painful to relive.

Something about Ally made him want to open up to her and that was dangerous. If she knew too much, it might frighten her away, and he wanted to be able to help her. He didn't want his past to push her away. Most of all, he didn't want to give her one more reason not to trust the Harmon name.

Ally watched Tucker hurry to his truck, then drive away. She made sure the front door was locked, then turned off all the lights, walked into the bathroom and shut the door. She leaned against it and breathed deeply as she felt color rising into her cheeks. She stared at her reflection in the mirror, then splashed her face with water.

She'd crossed a line with Tucker. His pain was buried deep and, for a brief moment, he'd shared it with her. She'd liked it, too—seeing a chink in his armor. It made him seem more human.

But he'd shut her out and he'd been right to do so. She hadn't come to Jessup to fall in love. She'd come for answers—answers that his family had conspired to keep from her. The fact that she was even trusting him to help her was ludicrous. He was a Harmon. The enemy. She'd promised herself that she would accept his help without getting involved with him.

Only Tucker had more than proven himself to her. She wouldn't pretend that she wasn't hurt by his rejection. She'd opened herself up to him. But he was right. Keeping any personal entanglement out of the equation was for the best. They couldn't afford to let emotion cloud their thinking.

Or else she might just fall for the man whose family had ruined her life.

Tucker checked in with his cousin and got the okay to use his system to do background checks on the employees of Harmon Ranch, as well as the people who'd been present when Ally was attacked.

So far, after hours of searching, he'd found no red flags.

A few of the ranch hands had minor infractions, arrests for fighting and racing, but nothing that would stand out to Tucker to make him think they would try to harm anyone. The delivery driver and the veterinarian were clean, too, and he checked out the backgrounds of the trainers and the mechanic for good measure.

Nothing.

He turned to the other lists he had. The one Ed had given him of the ranch employees around the time Tonya went missing and the list of names from witness statements from Police Chief Edwards's notes.

Once again, he found nothing. A few minor infractions but no major violent incidents or criminal charges.

It was time to change tactics and start interviewing people. He circled a name on the list. Someone who'd been at the ranch at the time Ally had been attacked and mysteriously disappeared before Tucker could speak to him.

The veterinarian, Dr. Ted Wilson.

He picked up his cell phone and dialed the veterinary clinic, only to learn that Dr. Wilson was on a call the next town over dealing with a breach cattle birth. The receptionist informed him he could be gone for hours and recommended another veterinarian he could use if his pet was having an emergency. He thanked her and hung up.

He could track down the doctor at whatever farm he was working at, but Tucker decided against that. If he was busy helping to birth a calf, any hesitation or irritation he might show at Tucker's questioning could be easily dismissed. No, he wanted to speak with the vet when his attention was all on him and Tucker could gauge his responses for himself.

Someone rapped on the door and Tucker turned to see his cousin enter the conference room where he was working.

"Finding anything useful?" Caleb asked.

Tucker sighed. "Not really."

"Unfortunately, I haven't, either." He held up several sheets of paper. "These are the forensic results from the pitcher you brought in and also fingerprint analysis from Ally's house. The pitcher did have traces of a sedative, but the sample couldn't be positively identified."

Tucker rubbed his chin. Traces of a sedative just confirmed that someone had been inside Ally's house and tried to harm her.

"The forensics team found no unusual fingerprints at her house, either. All of the samples we collected belonged to Ally Fulton. She's a teacher, so we have her prints on file to compare them to."

So they were at a dead end forensically.

With no video surveillance and no fingerprints or DNA, finding out who was attacking Ally was going to be more difficult than he'd thought.

Friday classes seemed to stretch longer than the normal hour per class. Ally couldn't blame the kids. They were their usual adolescent selves, excited to engage with one another but also looking forward to the weekend. It was difficult on good days to get them excited about Shakespeare's sonnets, but today had been especially tough. Ally could only blame her bad mood on the ongoing investigation. She was glad for Tucker's help, but the answers weren't coming. She'd hoped with his help, her mother's case would have been solved by now. And then there had been that awkward moment between them yesterday, when he'd opened himself up to her then unexpectedly retreated.

She was embarrassed that she'd tried to comfort him only to be pushed away, but blurring the boundaries between them would only complicate matters.

"Hi, Ally, how was your day?" Jenny Summers called to her and hurried over.

"Brutal," Ally confessed. "The end of the year won't get here soon enough for me."

"I know what you mean. I'm looking forward to starting my weekend. Rick and I are heading out of town to the beach. I'm looking forward to a few days of sunshine and waves."

Ally laughed with her friend. While she and her husband would be soaking up the sun, Ally would be returning into the dark world of murder in Jessup.

"What about you?" she asked. "Still digging into your mom's case?"

She nodded. Even if she wanted a vacation, she couldn't leave town with this case still being looked at. Who knew how long Tucker would be around to help her? "That's the plan. Enjoy your time off," she told her friend. "And tell Rick I said hi. You two have fun."

Ally waved to Jenny as she left the sidewalk and headed toward her car. She pressed the key fob to unlock it as she approached. Her phone rang and she pulled it from her pocket, smiling when she saw Tucker's name pop up. Her face warmed. There she went crossing those boundary lines again.

"Hello," she said into the phone as she answered the call.

"Hi there." His baritone voice sent shivers through her. "Are you through with school?"

"Yes, I was just walking to my car to head home."

"Well, I thought you might like an update. I finished doing background checks on all of our ranch employees and conducted some interviews. I've found some minor charges but nothing that popped up any red flags for me. And, Caleb told me, they didn't find any forensics or fingerprints that could help us. They found some traces of a sedative in the tea pitcher but nothing that's going to help us figure out who placed it there."

She sighed. "So we're still nowhere?" This news wasn't making her day any better.

"Maybe I can bring by dinner. We can look through what we have and try to figure out our next move."

She'd gotten used to seeing Tucker on most nights and she couldn't stop the smile that spread across her face. Ally opened her car door. "That sounds good." She tossed her backpack into the driver's seat just as her car suddenly burst into flames, the force of the explosion slamming her into the pavement several feet away.

She hit the ground hard and rolled as pain shot through her. Her ears were ringing but she heard Tucker's voice calling her and realized the phone had slipped from her hand and now lay on the ground a few inches away.

She twisted around. Her car was ablaze. People were running toward her.

Stunned, the magnitude of what had just happened suddenly hit her. Someone had set a bomb on her car. They had tried to kill her.

Again.

SEVEN

Tucker leaped to his feet as the sound of an explosion on the other end of the phone.

He called out to Ally again, but still hadn't heard her respond. His heart stopped for a moment at the idea that something terrible might have happened to her.

He hurried out of the conference room where Caleb had offered to let him work. He intended to alert his cousin about the explosion on his way out, but the excitement in the bullpen told him they already knew something had happened.

Caleb was shouting orders to his officers and coordinating the dispatchers when Tucker approached him.

"What is it, Tucker? We have an emergency." His tone had a bite to it and Tucker could tell he was stressed with the current crisis in his town.

"Explosion at the high school?"

Caleb shot him a questioning look. "You know?"

"I was on the phone with Ally when it happened. I think it was her car."

He nodded, then pushed Tucker toward the door. "Let's go."

He hopped into the passenger's seat of Caleb's SUV as his cousin started it. They sped through town, sirens blaring. Tucker tried to refrain from urging him to hurry. Caleb was already going at top speed, but for Tucker, it seemed like time had slowed. He tried Ally's phone again, but this time it went straight to voice mail. The sound of her scream mingled with the blast replayed in his mind as he gripped the dash in front of him. He wouldn't relax until he knew Ally was unharmed.

He saw the blaze before they'd even reached the parking lot and Tucker's gut clenched. Fire trucks and police vehicles surrounded the area. He had to hand it to Caleb's office. The first responders were on-site within minutes.

Caleb pulled up at to the scene and parked on the street. The police and fire department had the school parking lot blocked off and there was a crowd of people standing around watching and taking photos.

He spotted Hansen, one of Caleb's officers

that he recognized, and rushed to him. "Where is she? Did you see Ally?"

He shook his head. "No, we just arrived. I haven't seen her."

Tucker pushed past the crowd and toward the burning vehicle, which he recognized. It was definitely Ally's. He hurried around it, giving the blaze a wide range, scanning the parking lot for any sign of her.

He didn't breathe until he spotted her sitting up on a curb surrounded by several people. Someone was pressing a towel to her arm. "Ally!" He ran toward her.

She looked shaken up and pale, but she jumped to her feet and ran directly into his arms. "Oh, Tucker."

He pressed her against him, and suddenly the fear he'd felt at hearing the explosion over the phone reignited within him. If something had happened to her…

He shook off his own fears. He couldn't dwell on them. He had to remain strong for her sake and discover who was behind this and why.

First things first. He zeroed in on the piece of cloth tied on her arm. "Are you hurt?"

"Only some bumps and scrapes. I cut my arm on a piece of flying debris. I tossed my backpack onto the seat so I wasn't inside the car when it exploded."

He breathed a sigh of relief for that at least. "We need to get you looked at by the paramedics." He searched but saw the ambulance on the other side of the parking lot. He pulled out his phone and called Caleb. "Send the paramedics to the flagpole. Ally's been hurt. Nothing serious, but she's got a gash on her arm that needs to be bandaged."

She'd been very fortunate that it hadn't been worse. If she'd been inside the car at the time of the explosion, she would definitely have been killed.

An ambulance arrived and stopped near them. Tucker led her toward it and to the paramedics. "She was right near the explosion," Tucker told them. "Make sure she's checked over."

"Don't worry. We'll take care of her."

He stayed with her, watching as they stitched up her arm and checked her for a concussion. She denied losing consciousness after the explosion, but he couldn't imagine how she'd managed to escape with so few injuries when she'd been so close to the car at the time it exploded.

He glanced at the car still smoldering after the fire department had extinguished the flames. He shuddered at the thought of how close she'd come to dying.

His phone buzzed in his pocket and he pulled it out and glanced at the screen. "It's a text from Caleb. He wants me to come meet him."

She grabbed his arm. "You're not going anywhere, are you?"

He didn't want to leave her, but now that he knew she was safe, he wanted to know what had happened to cause this. "I'm going to go check in with my cousin. I want to know what they've found so far. I won't be far." He reluctantly left her and hurried back to his cousin, who was supervising everything. "Caleb, what have you found?"

He motioned him toward the fire chief. "Show us what you found," Caleb said.

The chief showed him a hunk of twisted metal. "We found this under the car. It's a homemade bomb. Looks like it didn't go off like it should have."

Tucker breathed a sigh of relief. If it had functioned properly, Ally would have been too close to the explosion to survive it.

"It was under her car and looks like it was set to go off once she got inside. There was a pressure plate beneath the driver's seat."

"Ally said she tossed her backpack into the seat. She never got inside."

"Good for her. This would have been a very

different conversation if she had gotten in, " Caleb said.

"Are there any identifiable marks on it?" Tucker asked the fire chief.

"No. It's composed of pretty common materials. The offender could have found these anywhere."

So they probably wouldn't be able to link the ingredients back to one person. He glanced around. "What about the video surveillance? I'm sure the school has cameras."

"I've already contacted someone to pull them," Caleb said.

Maybe those feeds would provide some answers. Someone would have to be desperate in order to sneak onto school property and plant a bomb. They had to know schools had surveillance for security reasons.

Caleb handed over his keys then nodded toward Ally still sitting on the back of the ambulance. "Why don't you go make sure she's okay. I'll handle this and catch you up once we have the video feeds."

Tucker had no choice. He wasn't law enforcement in Jessup, and even though Caleb knew him, the fire department didn't. They weren't going to allow a stranger to search through their fire scene.

He hurried back to Ally. "How are you feeling? Better?"

She was shivering with fear so he slipped his arm around her shoulders. "I just can't believe this happened. Why is this happening to me, Tucker?"

They both knew the reason. They were digging into the past that someone didn't want uncovered.

"Come on, Ally. I'll take you home."

She nodded and allowed him to lead her to Caleb's SUV. He opened the passenger's door and helped her inside, then closed it and hurried around to the driver's seat and started the engine. He reached across the seat for her hand as he turned onto the highway and headed toward her neighborhood.

He pulled the SUV into her driveway and they climbed out. She didn't have her keys so she punched in the number to the garage door and entered that way. Seeing the empty space where her car would usually be shook him. She'd come too close to being killed this time. The sound of the blast replayed in his mind and the fear he'd felt at not being able to reach her was something he wouldn't soon forget.

She fell into the chair in the kitchen and Tucker hurried to fix her a cup of hot tea to settle her nerves.

She sat quietly until the kettle whistled. "Who do you think did this?" she asked as he poured hot water from the kettle into her cup.

He shook his head. "I don't know. Hopefully, the video feeds from the school will capture them."

"Someone wants me dead, Tucker."

He slid into the chair opposite hers and held her hands. "We're going to find out who is behind this, Ally. We'll stop them."

Her hands were shaking and he did his best to provide her with some comfort, but she wouldn't be able to stop worrying about this threat until her attacker was behind bars.

He didn't want to leave her alone and she didn't seem bothered by him hanging around, so he ordered in takeout while she cleaned up. Then they vegged out on the couch and watched a movie.

As the sky outside darkened, he noticed her settling. She seemed calmer and he finally felt comfortable enough to leave her alone. She probably needed time to decompress on her own and didn't want a big, dumb cowboy hanging around.

"I'm sorry we didn't get around to looking at that information," she said as she walked with him to the front door.

"That's okay," he assured her. "They'll still

be there tomorrow." He stroked her cheek as a feeling of gratitude for her safety overwhelmed him. "I'm just glad you're okay."

"It's scary to think there's someone out there that wants me dead. It's unnerving."

"I know, but we'll catch whoever is behind this."

Still, he hesitated at the door. "Do you want me to stay? I can sleep on the couch."

At first, she seemed to like that idea, but then she shook her head. "That's not necessary. I'll be fine. I'll lock up and I promise to call if anything happens."

He stood at the door. Leaving was more difficult than he'd anticipated. He wanted to ensure she was safe, but he didn't know her well enough to intrude and insist. Besides, it wasn't his place. Home was supposed to be a safe place, but after the attacks against her, he doubted it still was.

"Good night," he told her, then turned away and walked down the sidewalk. He paused long enough to hear her lock the door behind him.

It felt wrong to go. Everything inside of him was telling him not to. He was probably still just shaken from Ally's near-death experience, but he knew sleep wouldn't come tonight. He climbed into the SUV and closed the door behind him. However, before he could turn the key in the ignition, he decided against it. Sleep was never going to come for him back at the ranch. All he'd be doing is worrying about her. He texted Caleb that he would be keeping his SUV overnight then he leaned back in his seat and settled in for the night.

Ally slept fitfully and awoke early with a headache. All of these attacks against her were beginning to take their toll. She'd come close to being killed yesterday and anything could have happened with that bomb. It could have killed someone else as well.

She walked to the kitchen to make coffee. Hopefully, the caffeine would help her stay awake and also aid in easing her headache. She turned on the coffee maker then glanced out the window.

Tucker was parked in her driveway. Had he pulled up without her realizing it? Or had he been there all night?

She didn't have to wonder. Her heart was warmed at the idea that he'd stayed to keep watch on her. She had very nearly accepted his offer to sleep on the couch, but she'd felt silly at the idea of having a babysitter.

She poured him a mug of coffee, then walked outside. He was leaned back against the headrest and looked like he'd dozed off. She wondered if he'd gotten any sleep at all during the night. She knocked on the window and he jerked awake, then looked at her sheepishly and rolled down the window.

"Morning," he said.

She smiled at the way his hair curled at the ends and he slicked it back with his hands.

"Good morning. I brought you some coffee." She handed him the mug, which he took.

"Thank you. I could use it."

"Have you been here all night, Tucker?"

He sipped the coffee then nodded. "It didn't feel right leaving."

He'd done so much to try to help her and protect her that she wasn't surprised by this action, but it did warm her heart. "Come on inside. We'll have some breakfast."

He nodded and got out, following her into the house. She fixed eggs and bacon while Tucker cleaned up in the bathroom. It wasn't as flashy a meal as he'd made her a few days ago, but she felt a satisfaction in watching him scoop it up and enjoy it.

"Did you get any sleep last night?" she asked him as they finished their meal.

He shrugged. "I've gone with less."

"You should go home and get some rest. I don't have anything planned for today. I need to order some groceries but I can have them delivered."

He shook his head. "I don't need sleep. I need to figure out who is behind these attacks on you. You're not safe until I do."

She shuddered and folded her arms. Goose bumps formed on her skin as she recalled how close she'd come to dying again yesterday. Actually, she had no choice but to have her groceries delivered, since her car had gone up in flames.

But that wasn't his problem. He'd already done so much. "Still, you need sleep."

"I'm fine, Ally. I'd much prefer to go do some interviews of people who were at the ranch when you were attacked. If you feel up to it, of course."

"Sure, I'm fine."

"Good, we can also pick up whatever groceries you need while we're out."

"And I need a rental car, too, since I can't drive mine anymore."

"Are you sure? I don't mind driving you around."

"I still have work. Besides, you might have something else to do when I need to go somewhere."

He grinned and sipped his coffee. "You might not have noticed, but I don't have a lot of obligations at the moment. I'm still technically on medical leave."

She wasn't used to being dependent on anyone. That was just the way she'd been raised. She was about to explain that to him when he suddenly shook his head.

"Never mind. If you'd feel safer with a rental car available to use, we'll swing by the rental agency and get you one. No problem."

"Thank you. That would make me feel better just for my own peace of mind."

She changed into jeans and a T-shirt, then grabbed her purse and followed Tucker outside. She made sure the doors were locked and the garage door was down before climbing into the SUV.

"So where are we headed?"

"Dr. Ted Wilson. Ed confirmed he was at the ranch when you were attacked. I was going to go by and interview him yesterday, but he had an emergency call in the next town." He pulled up an image on his cell phone and showed it to her.

She didn't recognize the man, but he appeared from his photo to be old enough to have been working when her mother was killed. She shuddered at the idea that he might be a killer before reminding herself that she didn't know that. Everyone she met was now a suspect.

He followed the GPS to the address listed on Dr. Wilson's website. Tucker parked the truck in the driveway of a small building with the words *Jessup Animal Clinic* written on the front. They got out and headed in. A bell jingled when Tucker opened the door and they stepped inside the small office.

A woman appeared at the front desk with a big smile. "Hi there. How can I help you today?"

"I'm Tucker Harmon. This is Ally Fulton. We were hoping to speak with Dr. Wilson about something that happened out at Harmon Ranch two days ago."

"Sure, I'll ask him."

She disappeared behind a door and Ally tried to concentrate on her breathing. She was suddenly very nervous about confronting this man. After several attacks, she now realized that her assailant could be standing right in front of her and she might not even know it. She couldn't trust anyone to be who they said they were.

Except Tucker.

She stared up at his commanding presence and felt safe enough to go through with this. She might not know whom to trust, but she trusted him completely. She looped her arm around his and he smiled at the gesture.

A man in scrubs greeted them and shook

Tucker's hand, then hers. "I'm Dr. Wilson. What can I do for you?"

Tucker took the lead. "You were at Harmon Ranch around nine a.m. on Thursday morning?"

He nodded. "Sure I was. Ed called me out to check on a horse with an abscess. While I was there, I gave a pregnant mare a good check-over, too."

"So you examined them inside the barn then?"

"The pregnant mare, yes. They were keeping her in the stables. However, I never got around to checking on the horse with the abscess. One of the ranch hands mentioned another horse that was favoring one hoof. I followed him to the corral to check on him first."

"So then you heard the gunshot and when the horses went crazy?"

He nodded. "Yeah, I heard that. The ranch hand that had led me there ran to see what was happening. I heard a commotion, but I stayed with the mare to keep her calm. She was getting a little spooked from the gunshot, too. He told me what had happened when he returned."

Dr. Wilson glanced at her. "You're the lady that was in there?"

Ally nodded. "Someone pushed me into that stall and intentionally spooked the horses."

"I'm sorry to hear that. I figured if someone

was hurt, I could help, but no one ever came to get me. I asked Ed about it later and he said you were shaken up but not injured."

"And then you abruptly left the ranch," Tucker said. "Why was that?"

Dr. Wilson seemed unfazed by the question. "I got an emergency call I needed to tend to. I went back by the ranch to check on the other horse earlier this morning."

"How long have you been the veterinarian for Harmon Ranch?" Tucker asked.

He shrugged. "I joined this practice fourteen years ago. They were already clients. They've been my client ever since."

"So twenty years ago? Where were you then?"

"College in Nebraska." Dr. Wilson continued. "I'm not originally from here. I moved here after vet school to accept a job from the former owner of this clinic, Dr. Ross. He retired six years ago and I bought him out."

Ally got a good feeling from Dr. Wilson and his story made sense to her. He hadn't even been in the state when her mother went missing, so it was doubtful he was involved in the attacks against her. She glanced at Tucker, but couldn't gauge his reaction.

He shook Dr. Wilson's hand. "Thank you for your time."

"No problem."

Tucker touched her elbow and led her outside.

"What do you think?" she asked him once they were out the door.

"I'll verify what he told us but I don't think he was involved. It does seem odd that he wouldn't come immediately if he thought someone might be hurt, but if the horse was antsy, that might make sense."

She agreed. "He didn't look at me like he wanted to kill me so I'm satisfied."

He chuckled. "Agreed." He started the SUV. "Let's head over to the feedstore. I want to talk to the delivery driver who was at the ranch when you were attacked. Then we'll head to the grocery store and the rental agency."

The feedstore was a bust since the delivery driver Tucker wanted to see wasn't working. He spoke to several of the others and learned that the head driver, Mike Crane, had gone out of town unexpectedly due to a family emergency.

Ally could see that information had Tucker on high alert. How convenient he was out of town right after Ally had been assaulted. It could be just a coincidence…or it could mean he was hiding out.

Tucker was tense as he joined her at Walker's Grocery Store. She limited her shopping to only the basic necessities she would need in the upcoming days. She could do a larger grocery order later in the week. Tucker loaded her bags into the back of the SUV, then drove her to the car-rental agency, where she arranged for a car to use. She drove the car back to her house while Tucker followed close behind.

Once back at her house, they put away the groceries, then ate and settled in for the night.

Ally found an extra blanket and pillow, then handed them to Tucker. "You're welcome to stay on the couch tonight."

He nodded. "That'll be a lot more comfortable than the truck."

"There's something I'd like to do tomorrow, Tucker."

He reached for her hand and held it. "Sure. Anything."

"I want to go to church."

His hand stiffened and he pulled it away. "Are you sure?"

She nodded. She'd been thinking about this since the car bomb had nearly killed her. She didn't want to die, but she especially didn't want to die without confronting her issues with God. "I'm sure."

He nodded. "Okay, then. We'll go to church."

She touched his cheek, then leaned in and kissed it. She also didn't want to die without letting Tucker know how much she'd come to care for him.

* * *

Tucker held the church door open for Ally as she entered in front of him. He removed his cowboy hat and smoothed down his hair as they headed toward the sanctuary. The church seemed much smaller to him than he remembered from attending during his childhood.

What was he doing back here? He regularly attended church in Dallas and enjoyed being of service to others. But today, he was here to support Ally. She'd claimed to have been away from church for a while and he could understand why. She'd suffered a great loss and had been denied answers about it for years. He'd seen people drift from their faith for much less.

He spotted Caleb, who was there with Penny and Missy. He waved them over so Tucker directed Ally in that direction. He made introductions, then slid onto the pew beside them.

The service was good and he enjoyed it. He saw tears stream down Ally's face and knew the sermon was affecting her, too. He'd fought for so long against returning to this town, to his family's ranch, but he'd finally just been beaten down to the point of needing to get away. The fallout from his last assignment with the Dallas PD had been a breaking point for him. He'd told himself he was distant enough from the pain in his life that coming back here wouldn't affect him, but he'd been wrong. Since being here, all the memories of his childhood, both good and bad, had come rushing back. He'd been trying so hard to push them away. He wasn't doing a very good job at it.

Now, he wondered if he'd gotten it all wrong. He'd hardened his heart for so long, refusing to let anyone in past all his pain and regret. Only Ally had gotten through his barriers. Had he been brought here for this reason? To help Ally? It was no coincidence that, for the first time in twenty years, they were both back in Jessup, Texas, a place neither one of them had ever planned to return to. It couldn't be. He didn't really believe in coincidences.

He felt her sobbing quietly beside him and his gut clenched. He wrapped his arm around her shoulder and pulled her close to him.

He didn't know why he'd been brought to Jessup and he didn't know if Ally could ever forgive his family or get past his family name, but he was determined to help her find the answers to what had happened to her mother twenty years ago.

And, if God was on their side, too, they couldn't lose, could they? Tucker would take all the help he could get.

* * *

Ally was thankful for Tucker's support. The sermon had moved her more than she'd anticipated. She'd been so angry at God for so long because God knew what had happened to her mom and He had yet to provide answers to her. She didn't realize how angry she'd been until the pastor began preaching on 2 Corinthians 5:7: "For we walk by faith, not by sight."

It hit her then that God owed her nothing. She'd been demanding her faith in response to Him providing her information, but that wasn't the way it was supposed to be. She should trust in God because of who He is, not because of what He could give her.

She'd been holding herself back instead of allowing God to heal her wounds, but today that truth had broken through. It was as if God had spoken to her through that Bible verse. That He wanted to be there for her. He wanted to comfort her during her time of grief and pain.

Tears streamed down her face as she finally surrendered.

God, I have faith in You. I don't know if You'll ever bring me the answers I seek about my mom's death, but I will follow Your guidance no matter what.

* * *

Tucker was happy to see Ally smiling as they gathered with Caleb and Penny after church ended.

"We're having everyone over for lunch," Penny told them both. "You two should come, too."

"Who is everyone?" Tucker asked. As far as he knew, Caleb and his family were the only ones living at Harmon Ranch besides him. Then he thought maybe she meant they were having something for the employees, like Ed had mentioned the family used to do.

Caleb answered his question. "Luke and Brett are coming to town this afternoon."

Tucker, Caleb and each of his other two cousins, Luke and Brett, had all inherited a portion of the ranch, but Tucker hadn't seen either of them or their families since coming to town. Caleb had told him they came in to stay often. Luke and his family used to live at the ranch before moving to Dallas, where he'd taken a job at Brett's security company.

However, it did strike him as odd that they were coming in on a Sunday instead of earlier in the weekend.

"What's the special occasion?"

"I have something I want to discuss with all

of you," Caleb said. "I wanted us all four to be together. As far as I know, they're not staying."

Now, he was curious. The only thing Tucker had in common with his cousins was this ranch and their childhood memories. Each of their fathers had died young and each death had torn the extended family apart.

He glanced at Ally, thinking she probably had no desire to return to the ranch after what had happened previously. However, when he looked at her, she was smiling. "I think it's a great idea," she told him. "I really like Penny and I'd love to get to know her better."

"Are you sure? What about what happened at the ranch before?"

She gripped his arm. "It'll be okay. I won't wander off on my own. Besides, I won't keep you from seeing your family again."

He finally agreed to take her, but as they made their way to the ranch, he gave her another chance to change her mind. "We don't have to do this, Ally. If you'd rather go home—"

"I wouldn't. I want to go. Besides, you need to see your cousins."

"I'm okay with not seeing them. I hardly know them."

Her tone turned serious as she looked at him. "Then you should take the time to get to know them, Tucker. Family is important and you still have some. You don't realize what a blessing that is."

He bit back an automatic, bitter reply. She was right. He'd been away from his family for so long and grown so cynical because of everything that had happened to him in his life. None of that was his cousins' fault. They'd each had their own hurdles to overcome in their lives. They'd each also lost their father at a young, impressionable age. That was something else they had in common.

He pulled into the driveway behind Caleb, Penny and Missy, and saw two other SUVs sitting in front of the house.

Tucker held Ally's hand as they walked inside and were met with a crowd of people he didn't really know. The big table in the formal dining room had been decorated and arranged with food containers. Hannah was calling out who should sit where. He looked at her and saw how her face was lit up. She finally had all the family under one roof again.

It felt wrong to feel out of place in his own family.

Two women came up and introduced themselves as Brett's wife, Jaycee, and Luke's wife, Abby. In addition, Abby pointed to two teenagers who were laughing along with Missy. It was obvious they all knew one another.

"It's nice to meet you both," Ally said, shaking their hands. "I'm Ally Fulton, a friend of Tucker."

Abby nodded. "Oh, yes, Luke told me. You're the one searching for her missing mother, is that right?"

"Yes. She used to work here at Harmon Ranch but she disappeared and she's never been found. Tucker has agreed to help me try to figure out what happened to her."

"I'm a reporter in Dallas and I used to work for the local TV news right here in Jessup," Abby told her. "Maybe we could get a segment done on your mom."

Ally's face lit up and she reached for Abby's hand. "That would be wonderful. I've been trying to get some traction on her story, but I haven't had any success." She glanced at Tucker before continuing. "It seems the Harmon name was always an obstacle."

He wondered if that would dissuade Abby, but she waved away that concern. "I grew up in Jessup. Believe me, I understand the power Chet Harmon had over this town but that's mostly faded away, especially now that he's gone. I'll call my former producer and see if we can arrange something."

Ally pulled her into a hug. "Thank you so much for your offer."

"I'm pretty good with computers," Jaycee told them. "Is there any way I can help?"

"I'm not sure." She glanced at Tucker, and he could see she was anxious for the help.

"I don't know, either," he said. "I've been doing background checks of everyone who was working at the ranch during that time. It hasn't been easy with the case being twenty years old. Ally also has an ancestry report that didn't take us anywhere."

"Why don't you send it to me and I'll see what I can do," Jaycee offered.

Abby nudged her cousin-in-law. "Jaycee is just being modest when she says she's good at computers. She's the cybersecurity expert for Brett's company. He and Luke both think she's amazingly talented."

Jaycee's cheeks reddened at the praise. "I can't make any guarantees."

"No," Tucker said. "Thank you. I'll send you what I have. It never hurts to have another set of eyes on the case."

He was grateful for their offers to help and seeing how happy it made Ally just made him appreciate these ladies all the more. Maybe family wasn't so bad.

"Let's all sit down and eat," Hannah called and everyone took their seats. "Ed, will you pray over our meal."

He hadn't noticed Ed and several of the ranch hands had joined them at the table. Ed said a prayer for thanks for the food and good company, then they all dug in. Tucker enjoyed himself more than he'd expected. He wasn't used to the loud noises and kids playing that surrounded him, but it wasn't an unpleasant experience. He realized Ally was right about being blessed with family. He hadn't given any of them a chance all because of the difficult life he'd lived. But life suddenly didn't seem so difficult to him at this moment. He owned a quarter of a large Texas ranch, had an extended family who'd welcomed him back and, best of all, he was sitting beside a pretty lady with a smile that lit up the room and a determination that inspired him.

The meal was over sooner than he would have liked.

Caleb pressed a hand to his shoulder and motioned for him. Tucker saw that Luke and Brett were with him, too, and figured he was about to learn why Caleb had called them all together.

He leaned over to whisper to Ally, "I'll be right back. Looks like Caleb is calling us all together."

She pressed her forehead against his. "Take your time. I'll be fine right here."

He didn't want to leave her, but Caleb had

made it seem like this meeting was important. Tucker followed them into a large study that his grandfather had used as an office. Caleb held the door as they all entered, then closed it behind Tucker who was the last one inside.

He turned to them all and took a deep breath. "I've asked you all here to talk about something important."

"What is it?" Luke asked him. "Is it about the ranch?"

"That's not all we have in common," Caleb said. "This is about Grandpa Chet."

Tucker stiffened at the mention. Everyone else in this room had made peace with their relationship with Chet. Tucker was the lone holdout. But perhaps they didn't know what Tucker now suspected—that their grandfather had a hand in covering up a murder.

"I recently received some disturbing new information about Grandpa Chet's death. A lab report that got misfiled."

"What kind of report? What did it show?" Tucker asked.

Caleb locked eyes with him. "It shows he was murdered."

Tucker stared at him in stunned silence for several moments, unable to make sense of what Caleb was saying. He glanced at his cousins' reactions. Luke stiffened and jumped to his feet while Brett sat still, unblinking. Both their expressions registered stunned shock.

"I don't understand," Luke said. "What do you mean he was murdered? He had a heart attack."

Tucker took the paper Caleb held out and scanned it. It showed a high level of digoxin had been found in Chet's body during his autopsy. "What is digoxin?" he asked.

Caleb had an answer for that, too. "It's a drug used to manage and treat certain heart conditions." He glanced at Luke to respond to his question. "It also has the ability to mimic a heart attack."

And Chet's official cause of death had been a heart attack. At least, that's what Tucker had been told when he'd been notified of Chet's death.

The silence between them was deafening as they all tried to make sense of this. Tucker's mind whirled with this new information.

Grandpa Chet had likely covered up Tonya Fulton's murder.

Then he'd been murdered, too.

EIGHT

"How long have you known about this?" Tucker demanded.

"A few months. I've been quietly performing my own investigation. I didn't mention it earlier because I didn't have any reason to think it was connected to Ally's mom's death. However, Tucker, when you mentioned to me that Grandpa Chet had been providing for Ally all through her childhood, it got me connecting the dots. He had to have been involved in her mom's disappearance."

Luke turned to him. "Wait, he provided for her?"

Tucker nodded. "He paid for her schooling and provided her aunt an income every month. He even purchased the house they lived in."

Brett folded his arms and leaned back on the couch. His initial shocked expression had morphed to anger at this new information. "It was more than he did for any of us."

"We all feel the same way," Caleb told him. "But we can't focus on that. I called you all here because, given this information, I think he must have had a hand in covering up what happened to Ally's mother. I don't believe he was a killer, but I can see him involved in a cover-up. I don't know why he would do that, but it makes sense that, if he did, maybe that's what got him killed."

"Just because you don't think he's a killer, Caleb, doesn't mean he didn't do it. There could have been an accident," Brett said.

"That's a possibility, but he had a lot of influence in town. Why wouldn't he just say it was an accident and let that little girl bury her mom?"

"Why did he do anything?" Brett demanded. "He had a temper. We all know it. If he was covering for someone, it had to be himself."

Caleb turned to Tucker. "You don't really believe Grandpa Chet killed that woman, do you?"

Tucker had to make a decision. He shook his head and handed the paper back to Caleb. "No, I don't think he killed her. From what I've uncovered, he cared about her. I do think, however, that he knew everything that happened on the ranch. At the very least, he covered up what happened. The police didn't do a proper investigation and Chief Edwards's widow says it was because Chet pressured the mayor not to."

Caleb's face reddened, but he didn't protest Tucker's summarization. "I can't argue with you about that. I'm just wondering if his murder has something to do with this woman's death."

"What do you mean?" Luke asked.

"Tucker is right. Grandpa knew everything that went on around the ranch. If that woman went missing, he had to know what happened. Why else wouldn't he have wanted a full investigation? From everything Tucker has uncovered, and what I've heard, he's always been loyal to his employees. This woman worked for him for years, then suddenly vanished and he started providing for her daughter." He shook his head. "There were rumors that she'd run off, but he had to know she wasn't coming back, which means he knew something had happened to her."

Brett spoke up. "So he covered for the killer all those years. Why do you think that got him killed? Surely there are others who had a reason to kill him?"

"I don't think so," Caleb offered. "Unfortunately, it seems like Grandpa Chet was generous with everyone except his family. He was a hard man but he engendered loyalty among his employees. I haven't been able to uncover any enemy he had."

"You know, Ed told me that a few years before he died, he found the Lord. He became a changed man," Luke told them. "Is it possible he decided he wasn't going to cover up for this person any longer?"

"And so whoever killed this woman killed Chet?" Tucker rubbed his chin as he considered that scenario. It made sense. "Ally had started digging into her mom's case around the time Grandpa Chet died. She'd reached out to him, asking him to help her. Maybe his guilty conscience finally got to him and he was going to come clean and tell her everything, and the killer didn't like it."

"But how do we prove who that was?" Brett asked.

Caleb sighed deeply. "It would have had to have been someone who could get close to Chet. Someone who still had access to him or to the ranch."

Luke's face paled at that scenario. "Someone who's still around the ranch."

Tucker knew many of the ranch's employees had been there for decades. "Ally was attacked while she was here. Whoever he is, he was here days ago."

"Hannah and Ed have both been there for

more than thirty years and were closer to him than anyone else," Luke mused.

Caleb glared at him for even suggesting it. "Hannah's no killer."

"I can't believe Ed is, either," Luke argued.

Tucker thought back on his conversations with Hannah about Tonya Fulton. "I questioned Hannah about Ally's mom's disappearance. She spoke kindly of her. I don't think she would harm anyone, but she definitely could have gotten close enough to Chet to poison him. She was the one in charge of his food."

Caleb shook his head. "I can't believe Hannah would harm anyone, much less Grandpa Chet. She's been a faithful employee for years. I just won't believe it."

Then Tucker recalled something Hannah had said. "She met her husband Charlie around the time that Tonya vanished. If he was involved—"

"He's dead," Luke interrupted. "He died long before Grandpa Chet. Even if he killed Ally's mom, why continue to protect him now by killing Chet? They had no kids together. No reason to still shield him." He shook his head. "That would be hard to believe."

Tucker shrugged. "Maybe she was protecting her reputation. She didn't want to be known as the wife of a killer." He didn't want to believe it either but they had to consider all scenarios.

Brett held up his hands to stop them all. "We can keep going in circles with this. We need proof, not speculation." He motioned toward the lab report. "What does that report show? How close would the killer have had to get to Chet?"

"Close," Caleb responded. "The autopsy didn't show any signs of an injection, but I spoke with the new medical examiner and she said the drug would likely have to have been injected or a big dose swallowed to work as fast as it did."

"Statistically, women are more likely to use poison to kill than men," Luke said.

Caleb rubbed his head, frustrated. "Hannah has been like a mother to me. I know she's not capable of this. And Charlie was a good man. I never suspected him of any wrongdoing." He blew out a breath and he acknowledged the truth. "I never suspected anyone at Harmon Ranch was capable of murder. I'm the chief of police and apparently this happened in my own home right under my nose. How could I have missed it?"

"Everyone did," Brett reminded him. "The autopsy came back with natural causes. You had no reason to be suspicious. None of us did."

"The question is what do we do now?" Luke asked. "Caleb, you said you've been quietly investigating this and haven't come up with anything solid to point to anyone. Why are you telling us about it now?"

"Because I believe it is related to Tucker's investigation. I think if we discover who killed Ally's mom, we'll find out who killed Chet, too. Luke is right. About a year before he died, Grandpa Chet gave his life over to Jesus. He was changed. Even I could see it. Tucker, you said that's about the same time that Ally's aunt died and she began looking into her mother's disappearance. I know she reached out to Chet. I saw some of her letters. I think he was going to tell her the truth. I think he was going to stop covering for whoever harmed her mom."

"So the killer had to stop him," Luke inserted.

Caleb nodded. "And, since Chet was loyal above all, he would have given this employee the chance to come clean on his own."

Tucker nodded. It made sense and was a good lead to follow.

"Whatever help you need, I'm available," Luke offered. "I'm staying in town until we figure this out."

"Me, too," Brett stated. "Jaycee can ride back to Dallas with Abby and the kids. We'll stay and help you investigate this."

Tucker was suddenly glad to have his cousins on his side. "Both of your wives have already offered their help, too," he told them. "They seem nice."

"They are," Luke agreed. "So is Penny," he said, turning to Caleb. He looked at Tucker, too. "And I really like Ally. She deserves to find out what happened to her mom."

"She's been battling the Harmon name for years. Grandpa Chet used his influence to take something important away from her."

Luke nodded. "Then we'll just have to use the Harmon name to give it back to her."

Caleb nodded. "We will figure this out. We will find out who killed Ally's mom and, in doing so, find Grandpa Chet's killer, too."

Tucker was glad to have his cousins firmly on his side. "I'm not going to mention this to Ally," he told them. "She's been through a lot in the last few days with the attacks against her. Finding out that Grandpa Chet was going to give her the answers she wanted, only to have that opportunity taken from her by the same man now trying to killer her...well, I don't want to hurt her again."

Caleb's face turned grim. "I'm going to dig into Charlie's background. I don't believe he would have been involved, but at this point, I'm not ruling anything out."

Tucker knew his cousin was in a precarious spot. He'd lived most of his life on Harmon

Ranch. Everyone who worked here was like his own family. And now, he was digging into the deepest crevices of their lives in order to find a killer.

Ally enjoyed listening to Abby tell stories about her kids' antics. She laughed about the joys of being a mom and Ally could see how much she loved her life and her family.

"Do you miss Harmon Ranch?" Ally asked her.

She nodded. "I miss Jessup sometimes. This is, after all, where everything started with Luke and me. I spent so many years trying to get away from this town and so did he, but when we lived here at the ranch, it was good. It's good where we are now, but it's a different kind of good. It's a new adventure for our family."

Jaycee put her arm around Abby. "Well, we're glad to have you in Dallas. Brett and I are really enjoying having family around."

Ally loved the bond that had formed between the two women.

Penny and Hannah entered carrying a plate of brownies and placed them on the table. "Time for dessert," Penny exclaimed.

Ally had seen firsthand how close Penny and Hannah were, too, and she suddenly found herself envious of the family bonds these people had created. It had been a long time since she'd had people she could depend on… Not since Aunt Kay had died.

A door slammed and she spotted the men returning. Tucker's jaw was clenched as he approached them.

"Are you okay?" she asked as he reached for a brownie and bit into it.

He grabbed her hand. "Let's go do something fun."

She followed him, allowing him to pull her outside. "What are we doing?"

He stopped and turned to her, and she could see the stress etched in his expression. She touched his cheek. "What happened up there? What did Caleb want to tell you?"

He covered her hand with his own. "Nothing. It's not important. Do you want to take a ride with me?"

She glanced toward the barn, where she'd been shoved into the stall, and felt the urge to flee.

Tucker held her arms. "I know, I know—the barn. We'll get the horses and take a ride down by the lake. I could use some time to decompress."

She was still frightened, but didn't want to disappoint him. "I haven't been on a horse in a long time, Tucker. Not since I was a kid." Except for the few minutes she'd ridden with him after being shot.

"It's okay. I'll be right there with you. We can ride together."

She would feel better with him taking the reins but she was still hesitant. However, if he needed this, she was glad to go with him. Finally, she agreed.

They walked down to the barn and Tucker had a horse saddled in a matter of minutes. He slid into the saddle then reached for her and helped her climb on behind him. She wrapped her arms around his waist and pressed herself against him. Fear of being on horseback for the first time in years melted away at the feel of his strong presence, and the scent of his aftershave tickled her nose. She trusted this man. He wouldn't let anything happen to her.

Tucker headed through the pasture. He started off easy and Ally found herself relaxing and enjoying the landscape. Harmon Ranch really was beautiful.

After they'd ridden for a while, he pulled the horse to a stop near a small lake. The sunshine shimmered across the water. It was pretty. Suddenly, a memory clicked into place.

"I remember this place," she told him, sliding off the horse.

He climbed down, too, and followed her as she ran toward the water's edge.

She smiled at the sweet memories that suddenly flooded her mind. Good times with her mom. "Mama and I used to come down here all the time. I used to swim and she would sit on the bank and read a book. I used to like to splash her. I wanted her to come into the water with me but she never wanted to get her hair wet."

Then a much more sinister memory pushed the other images aside.

A day at the pond swimming and reading like any other normal day. Ally had gone under the water. A scream. She'd resurfaced and saw a man hovering over her mom, something shiny in his hand. Shiny and red.

Ally screamed, too, and the man looked at her then came after her. She scrambled from the water on the other side of the bank and took off running back toward the big, red barn in the distance. She looked back, seeing her mother lying unmoving on the grass and knowing that something was very wrong.

Tucker grabbed her arm, pulling her back to the present. "Are you okay? You suddenly look very pale."

She sucked in a breath. Her heart was pounding a mile a minute. She looked up into his concerned green eyes and shook her head. She was definitely not all right. "It just hit me."

"What did?"

"A memory of the day my mom died. We were here, Tucker. We were here at the lake. I was swimming. She screamed as a man grabbed her. He chased me from the water. I remember it." She'd locked that day away for so long that she'd begun to think it was never going to be recovered. She *had* been there when her mother was killed. She'd witnessed it happening.

Anxiousness mixed with a hint of excitement appeared on Tucker's face. "You saw the man who killed your mom?"

She stared at Tucker and blinked as she tried to capture the memory again. She had seen him but… "I—I didn't really see his face."

"What do you mean you didn't see his face?"

"I mean, I don't remember his face." It hit her then like a ton of bricks. This terrible memory would be of no help in identifying her mother's killer. All it would do was to traumatize her all over again. "I can't identify him."

She could see he was as disappointed as she was, but he nodded and rubbed his chin. "Maybe it'll come to you. You didn't think you would remember this much. Maybe the rest is coming."

She didn't think so, but like he said, she hadn't expected to recall this much.

A wet drop hit her cheek then she heard one hit Tucker's hat. She glanced up as a sudden downpour of rain drenched them both.

They returned to the horse and Tucker grabbed the reins. "I saw an equipment storage shed just over the hill," he said. "We can take shelter there." He grabbed her hand and they darted toward it, pulling the horse behind them.

He pushed open the door and she ran inside, glad to be out of the rain as Tucker pulled the horse into the shed with them. That had been unexpected. She slipped off her jacket and wrung out the water. Tucker removed his cowboy hat and water poured from it.

"We can wait it out in here. It shouldn't last long."

She shivered, but she wasn't sure if it was more from being cold from the downpour or the memory she'd just recovered. It could be either. Tucker found an old towel and quickly wiped down the saddle. He walked to one side of the shed and found a heater, which he turned on. "Come over here and get warm."

Ally walked to the heater and stood in front of it. At least it would help dry her off. After a few minutes, she sat down on the concrete floor. "What is this place?"

There were boxes stacked in a back corner and tractor equipment. "Looks like a machine shop. I don't remember it being here, so I'm glad I noticed it when we passed by." He took a seat beside her and leaned against the wall.

Then came the tears as the horribleness of what she'd recalled hit her. She'd been trying too hard for so long to recover those memories and now she would give anything to make them go away again.

Tucker slid his arm across her shoulder and inched closer to her. She was thankful he didn't try to make her stop. She wasn't even sure she could. The vision of seeing the glint of the knife and the color of the blood sent tremors through her.

"I'm sorry," she said, sniffing back tears once she was able to.

"You have no reason to be sorry," he assured her. "What you remembered had to have been terrible."

"I wish I could unsee it. I wish I could take it back." Especially now that she knew that remembering it would do nothing to help solve the mystery of who'd taken her mother from her.

"I know. I wish you could, too."

"I remember running toward the barn. I could see it in the distance. A big, red beacon of safety. I remember thinking that. Only I went and hid in the stalls and the man never came to find me. I wonder why." She shuddered as she recalled the terror she'd felt that this man had hurt her mother and was going to come find her and hurt her, too.

"He might have run into someone along the way. Whoever it was probably saved your life."

She sniffled. "You're probably right. Until now, all the memories I'd recovered of the ranch were good and fun memories from my childhood. Now, that's all ruined."

He sighed. "I have good memories of this place, too. When I was a kid, this was one of my favorite places to be. We fished, hunted, took care of the horses. It was a little kid's dream life. At least, that's the way it seems to me now."

"What happened?"

"My father died. He was killed. He was helping some neighbors clean up after a bad storm and accidentally came across a live power line. He was electrocuted and died instantly. After that, everything changed. My grandfather had already lost two of his sons—and Caleb's dad would also die just a year later—so he was understandably devastated. We all were. But my grandfather became a different person, angry and bitter. I don't know why, but he couldn't even look at me and my mom. I guess it was too hard for him. Without my dad, she struggled to put food on the table. I know she asked him for money. I remember hearing her on the phone begging him to help her. He never did."

"How did you two survive?"

"She did what she could to scrimp by, but she ultimately ended up marrying my stepdad. I guess she thought he was going to help us get back on our feet, but he was abusive and our lives went from bad to worse. I left home when I was sixteen and never went back. I was so angry at everything. At my mom for staying married to that guy, at my stepfather for being a louse and especially at my grandfather. I blamed him for all of it. If he'd just helped us, she might never have married that guy."

She remembered the terrible story he'd told her about his mom killing his stepfather and how he hadn't been able to help her.

A tear slipped from his eye and he quickly wiped it away and took a deep breath, obviously trying to regain his composure.

"I'm sure she knew you loved her."

"I spent the next years just drifting with no rudder until I found a mentor who led me in the direction of law enforcement. It was one of the best decisions I ever made. But now... I don't know what's going to happen with my life or my career." He chuckled. "When I first got here, I was restless, ready to be back on the job. Now, I don't even know if I want to return. I'm starting to like it here. Maybe I'll just stay in Jessup and become a rancher."

She liked the idea that he might stick around town.

"What about you?" he asked. "Do you like being a teacher?"

She smiled and was glad to find a happy memory to hang on to. "I do. I had a teacher who helped me a lot after my mom died and my whole world was turned upside down. Suddenly, I was living with my aunt in a new town and going to a new school. Everything was different. But my teacher at my new school was very encouraging and very kind. She made me want to do the same for other kids. It seemed a natural choice and I enjoy the students. It's not always easy, especially with middle schoolers, but I like it."

"Do you think you'll stay even after you find out what happened to your mom?"

"I wasn't planning on it. I thought I would take this job and be here for at the maximum a year while I searched for answers. However, I like the school, I like the town and I'm not sure what I really have to go back to."

"I guess both our futures are up in the air."

"Or, maybe, the future is whatever we make it."

She sucked in a breath and turned to stare

out the window at the rain still battering down. Were they really sitting here talking about the future? It seemed too soon. She'd only known Tucker for a week, yet in that time, she'd come to rely on him more than any other person in her life. She enjoyed being with him and could no longer deny the urge to get lost in his eyes.

She pressed herself against him as they sat on the floor, her head against his shoulder and his arm around her as the rain pelted the metal roof. His breathing was steady and calming, but she'd never felt more protected than she did in this moment.

It was too soon when he spoke again. "Looks like the rain has stopped." He stood and walked to the window. "We can head back now if you're ready."

She wasn't ready. Her face warmed as she realized she could have remained wrapped in his arms all day. Instead, she stood and dusted off her jeans. "I'm ready."

Tucker held the door open for her, then led the horse out. The sun was now shining, but the ground was still wet and the air held a sweet smell to it.

Tucker cupped his hands as he motioned to her. "I'll lift you into the saddle."

She placed one hand on his shoulder and her foot into his palms. He lifted her easily to the right height and she grabbed hold. However, her foot slipped as she pushed it over the saddle and she lost her balance, falling backward.

Tucker caught her before she hit the ground, his strong arms surrounding her, making her feel safe and protected from something as simple as falling off a horse. In the same way he made her feel safe and protected from the man who was trying to end her quest for answers about her mother.

His face was close to hers as she stared up at him. He tensed and his eyes fell to her lips. It seemed like he wanted to kiss her and all the air surrounding her evaporated from her lungs at the thought. She wanted it, too, and she prayed he wouldn't stop himself again.

He didn't. He lowered his head and put his lips on hers, his strong arms pulling her tight against him as his hands found their way through her hair. It felt good and right kissing him and being in his arms. More true than anything else in her life had felt in a long time.

He broke away from her, his cheeks coloring and his head lowering sheepishly. "I'm sorry. I shouldn't have done that." But even the grit in his voice belied his apology.

"I'm not sorry," she told him, surprising even herself at her boldness. When his eyes widened in surprise, and then a smile tugged at his lips, she stroked his jaw. "I liked it. I like you, Tucker. I'm tired of fighting it."

His grin spread wide and his shoulders relaxed. His finger caressed her cheek. "I'm glad to hear it. Because I like you, too, Ally, and I'm tired of fighting it."

He kissed her again then lifted her back onto the horse. She wrapped her arms around his waist when he climbed on and she was floating on cloud nine as they made their way back to the farmhouse.

NINE

Tucker spent the night on Ally's couch again, then drove her to work Monday morning. She had her rental car in the garage, but he wasn't taking any further chances on someone tampering with it again. So far, the school's video feeds hadn't provided any suspects. Whoever had planted the bomb under her car had known how to avoid the cameras.

"Are you sure you don't want to take a few days off?" he asked her as he pulled up to the school's front entrance.

"I need to be here," she reassured him. "Most of the kids had already left campus on Friday when the bombing happened, but they will have heard about it on the news or through social media. They need to see that I'm okay…and I am okay."

He was glad she'd added that last reassurance. He needed it, too. He admired her courage and her determination to do what was right for her students. "I'll pick you up at three thirty. Have a great day." He wished he could camp out in her classroom to make certain no one bothered her, but the school had rules against visitors during school hours. Besides, he figured she would be safe inside for the day. Caleb had been in touch with the principal and made arrangements for the school's security to be increased. Also, since the car bombing, the staff were all being put on alert for suspicious activity.

She leaned over and kissed him, then got out and hurried into the building. He watched until she was safely through the doors, then turned around and drove to the police station. Caleb had asked him to swing by so they could go over the evidence they'd collected from the car bombing and the other attacks against Ally. He was surprised to see Brett and Luke there as well, but he shouldn't have been. They'd remained in town to investigate Grandpa Chet's murder and help him out with Ally's investigation.

"Any updates?" he asked Caleb.

"Nothing significant. The fire chief sent me a preliminary report on the bomb beneath Ally's car. All of the components were easily attainable and nothing special about them. We won't be able to trace their origins."

Tucker rubbed the back of his neck. "This assailant is smart. He doesn't take chances. It'll make him more difficult to find, but Ally won't be safe until we do."

"What's your next step?" Brett asked Tucker.

"I have a list of names Ed gave me of people who worked at the ranch when Ally's mom went missing as well as a list of people working there now. I performed criminal background checks on everyone but I wouldn't mind a second pair of eyes in case I missed something."

"We can help with that," Luke stated and Brett nodded.

"I'm also reaching out to Bill Collins, the accountant for Harmon Ranch. I'm hoping there might be payroll or employee records from that time still available."

Caleb shook his head. "After twenty years, that's doubtful."

"I know, but I need to check."

Luke backed him up. "A lot of places were already digital back then. If they were, it's possible they have backups from that time."

Tucker hoped that was the case. He knew this was a longshot, but he needed to know everything he could about the people who were at Harmon Ranch when Tonya Fulton went missing. He just felt like he was digging endlessly for answers.

"There's something else. Ally's memories of that day came back to her. She witnessed her mother being stabbed to death."

Each of their faces conveyed the appropriate shock at how traumatizing that must have been for her.

"Can she identify the attacker?" Caleb asked hopefully.

"No. She didn't see his face. Unfortunately, she didn't remember anything that will help us find her mother or the killer."

"That's disappointing," Brett said. "What about cadaver dogs? We could search the property."

Luke shook his head. "That would take forever. We have no idea where on the ranch she was buried, or if she even was. Whoever attacked her could have placed her into a vehicle and dumped her body somewhere else."

"What about cell phone or computer tracking?"

Caleb shook his head. "According to the police file from the time, Tonya didn't own a cell phone. This was twenty years ago. They hadn't really become popular yet. Her computer was recovered, but nothing was found on it so the police returned it to Grandpa Chet. Who knows where it is now."

Tucker clenched his jaw in frustration. That

police file still irritated him. It seemed to only contain enough information to prevent them from finding anything.

Luke stood. "Well, I know one thing for sure. Grandpa Chet had a cell phone when he died. I'm going to pull those records and find out where he went and who he interacted with in the days prior to his death. Maybe that'll give us some clue or lead to follow."

Tucker nodded. "That's a good idea." If they were right and whoever had killed Ally's mom had also murdered Grandpa Chet, finding his killer would also lead them to Tonya Fulton's killer.

Brett stood. "I'll get started on these background checks. I'll let you all know if I uncover anything."

Tucker was grateful for all the help from his cousins. "I'm heading over the accountant's office now. Text me if you find out anything," he told Caleb.

He exited, climbed into his pickup and keyed the accountant's address into the GPS. He'd phoned him first thing this morning and was anxious to hear if he'd found anything.

He arrived at the office and a pretty receptionist led him into Mr. Collins's office. Tucker removed his cowboy hat, then reached for the hand of the man behind the desk. "Mr. Collins,

I'm Tucker Harmon. I spoke with you on the phone earlier."

"Yes, come in, Mr. Harmon." He motioned for Tucker to have a seat, then went back behind his desk. "It's nice to meet you. I've had the honor of meeting your cousins, but not you before."

"I just arrived in town a few weeks ago."

"Well, congratulations on your inheritance. I've been to the ranch. It's beautiful."

Tucker couldn't argue with that. As much as he'd wanted to dislike the place, he didn't. It was beginning to feel like home. "Thank you. Were you able to find anything about the issue I called about?"

"Yes, I did. As you know, our firm has handled your grandfather's estate for over forty years. Chet Harmon was my father's very first client when he started this firm."

"I didn't know. How about that."

"We don't normally keep payroll or tax records that long, however my father was something of a pack rat. We digitized some of our files so I sent my receptionist to the storage area after our conversation. She was able to find our backups from that year."

That sounded like he'd caused them a lot of work. He hoped it wasn't going to amount to nothing.

"I went back to the year you requested and I was able to find those records. Comparing them with the list you emailed me, I found a discrepancy." The accountant handed a file folder to Tucker, so he opened it and scanned through it, but the number of pages was overwhelming.

"What did you find?" Tucker asked instead.

"An employee who was listed among the payroll records twenty years ago. However, he was not on the list of employees you gave me."

Probably just an error on Ed's part. It couldn't be easy to remember everyone who'd worked at the ranch twenty years earlier. "Who was it?"

"A man named Tyler Grey. He worked off and on at the ranch for many years. The name stood out to me."

"Why did it stand out to you?"

"Because I know him. Tyler Grey worked as a ranch hand years ago, but he's a land developer now and a pretty prominent one, too. He owns his own construction business and we played together on our church's golf retreat last year."

Tucker jotted down the name. One more person to interview about his time working at Harmon Ranch. He doubted it would result in anything, but they still had to check it out.

"And you're sure he was working there around this time?"

Collins shrugged. "Well, he received a paycheck every week up until the summer. Then again in September and October of that year. Looks like he was off and on after the spring of that year."

Tonya had disappeared in April of that year, which meant Grey was working at the ranch during that time period, but his tendency to come and go could explain why Ed hadn't recalled him working during that time.

Tucker stood and shook Mr. Collins's hand. "Thank you for this information and for locating these employee files. I, for one, am glad your father was a pack rat."

"Well, it's good timing on your part. I'm retiring in a few months and closing the business. All those files would have been tossed out except for the ones the law mandates we keep. Those will be sent to whoever you all decide to handle your accounts from now on."

He had no idea who was even making that decision, but if he intended to keep his share of Harmon Ranch, he would want to know those details. And he couldn't deny the timing was favorable. He didn't believe in luck, but he wasn't ready to say it was God's guidance, either, that had brought them together. Although, he couldn't deny they were at the right place at the right time. Again.

That had to be more than a simple coincidence.

He wished Mr. Collins well then left his office. He hopped back into his truck and glanced at the clock. Ally would still be in class, but he couldn't wait to find answers about this new development. He wanted to have a conversation with Tyler Grey and decide whether or not he could be ruled out as Ally's mom's attacker. Mr. Collins might have found it odd that he'd been left off of Ed's list, but Tucker didn't find it especially suspicious. Twenty years was a long time ago and Ed wasn't getting any younger.

Tucker drove back to the ranch to wash up and grab lunch. While he was there, he spotted Hannah folding a load of towels.

"How's it going?" she asked with a big smile. She was doing her best to make him feel at home and he appreciated that.

"Good, good. I just got back from obtaining some records from Mr. Collins."

"The accountant? I'd heard he was retiring and taking up golfing full-time."

"He is, but not for a few months. I guess he has some strings he still needs to tie up."

"What kinds of records were you looking for, Tucker?"

"Employment records. I wanted to know the

names of everyone who worked on the ranch during the time Tonya disappeared."

"I thought Ed gave you those names."

"He did. I was just double-checking. Only he left one off. Tyler Grey. Do you remember him?"

She nodded and turned back to her laundry. "Sure, I remember Tyler. He showed up at the ranch years before looking for work. I remember he was a scrawny kid. Looked like he wasn't hardly fifteen years old. We all suspected he'd run away from home."

"Only no one called the police?"

"From the way he talked, home was a dangerous place to be. I remember Ed took him under his wing and taught him about ranch work. He grew up to be a fine young man. He would set off on his own, get into trouble, then head back here and Ed would hire him back for a while until he got back on his feet again."

"How long did that go on?"

"Tyler was a fixture around here for several years."

"Do you think Ed remembers him?"

"Of course, he does. I told you. He was like a father to that boy."

"Then why would he forget to add him to the list of employees I asked for?"

She shrugged. "Maybe he didn't remember

he was working here at the time you asked. Like I said, he was coming and going quite a lot until he finally landed on his feet. He discovered he was good at construction work. He finally found a job that he enjoyed and could do. I hear he owns his own contracting company now."

Tucker rubbed his chin as he mulled over her words. She was probably right. It probably had slipped Ed's mind. He would have no reason not to include him if he'd been on the payroll back then. But learning that Ed had been so close to this Tyler Grey, and had neglected to include him on Tucker's list, raised a red flag. He hadn't really been suspicious before, but now he was even more anxious for this interview.

He thanked Hannah, then headed upstairs to his room. He needed to go through those payroll records and see what he could find. Hopefully, something in there would lead him in a different direction.

But, before he did, he hopped into the shower and changed clothes. He didn't mind sleeping on Ally's couch, but he didn't feel right showering there or bringing clothes. That felt too intimate and, despite how close they'd grown, that struck him as crossing a line.

He grabbed a sandwich from the kitchen then hopped back into his pickup and headed to the address he'd looked up for Tyler Grey's construction company. He might as well get that interview out of the way before he had to pick up Ally from school.

Tucker drove across town after stopping by the office of Tyler Grey's company and learning he was currently working on a construction site.

Tucker pulled up to an area gated off and parked. He got out and asked around for Grey. Someone pointed him toward a man in a hard hat who appeared to be in charge.

The man spotted Tucker and waved him over. Tyler Grey was in his midforties, with a wide smile and tanned skin. He held out his hand. "Tyler Grey. My office called and said you were coming by. What can I do for you?"

"My name is Tucker Harmon."

Recognition showed in his face. "Harmon? You're one of Chet's grandsons?"

He nodded. "Yes, that's right. I understand you used to work at the ranch?"

He took off his hat and rubbed his head. "A long time ago." He slipped his hat back on. "I was sorry to hear about your grandfather."

"Thank you. I'm revisiting everyone that was working or living on the ranch twenty years ago."

"What about?"

"Do you remember a woman named Tonya Fuller?"

He thought for a moment then shook his head. "The name doesn't ring a bell."

"She used to work at Harmon Ranch as a bookkeeper. She went missing twenty years ago."

"Oh, sure. Now I know who you mean. I remember when that happened."

"Were you working at the ranch during that time?"

"I wasn't. If I recall, I'd recently started working in town at the tractor supply store when she went missing. Of course, everyone in town knew about it. It was big news at the time."

"So you didn't know her?"

He shook his head again. "No, not really. I mean, she worked at the ranch while I was there but we never had much interaction. She did the books and I did the grunt work. What's this about? They're not reopening that case, are they?"

"We are. Her daughter is back in Jessup and looking for answers. She deserves to know what happened to her mom, don't you think?"

He shrugged but Tucker couldn't get a good read from him. "Sure. I guess I never thought about that."

"I understand you and Ed, the ranch manager, were close."

He nodded. "Ed was good to me. He took a kid from a troubled home and tried to give me a purpose. He's a good man."

"Do you ever see him now?"

"No, I haven't seen him in years. I probably should take him a fruit basket or something. If he hadn't stayed on me and helped me so much when I was younger, I probably wouldn't be where am I today—a successful member of society." He motioned toward the construction site where they were. "I'm overseeing multiple sites like this one in the tri-county area and I'm looking to expand throughout the state."

Tucker had never cared much about wealth, but he admired the man's hard work. But he had a job, too. "Was there anyone at the ranch that you remember that might have been a danger to Tonya?"

He thought for a moment then shook his head. "Not that I can recall. It's been a long time and, in those days, people came and went all the time."

"What about Ed? Could he have had a hand in her disappearance?"

Grey chuckled, then shook his head. "Even twenty years ago, long before he found his religion, Ed wouldn't have hurt a fly."

That was good to hear and helped ease Tucker's mind about Ed. He shook Grey's hand. "Thanks for your time. I appreciate it."

"No problem. I hope you find whoever did that."

Tucker glanced at his watch as he walked back to his truck. Another interview down with no more answers than he'd had before. Grey claimed not to have been working at the ranch when Tonya went missing, but it had been so long ago and, according to the payroll records, he'd left soon after. Time had a way of muddling memories so he wasn't sure he could prove any malicious intent on either Ed's or Grey's part for not remembering exact dates. He needed more.

Only Hannah's insistence that Ed had been like a father to Grey still gnawed at him. He needed to straighten this matter out once and for all.

He drove to the ranch and parked his pickup at the barn. He called out to Ed, who shouted back from his office. Tucker followed his voice and found Ed at work behind his desk.

"Tucker, what have you been up to?" he asked.

"Nothing much. I just returned from interviewing Tyler Grey." He watched Ed for any reaction, but the older man remained cool and composed.

"Tyler? Why'd you go see him?"

"Because he was one of the employees at Harmon Ranch during the same time period that Tonya Fuller disappeared."

Ed shook his head. "No, I don't believe Tyler was working here at that time. He'd taken a job in town as I recall."

"He said the same thing when I interviewed him. Only, Mr. Collins, the accountant, was able to find payroll information showing that he was being paid by the ranch—by you—at the time she went missing." He pulled out a sheet of paper showing an electronic deposit made out to Tyler Grey and dated the same week Ally's mom vanished. There were also six more deposits afterward. "He was definitely working here, Ed. Either that, or you were paying him for something he wasn't doing."

Ed seemed to take offense to that accusation. He took the printout Tucker had and glanced at it before returning it to him. "I guess I was mistaken about the dates."

He tried to shrug it off, but Tucker could see in his face that it wasn't an honest mistake. Ed had a sharp mind and he'd known what he was doing. That angered Tucker. He wanted to know why. "I don't believe you were mistaken,

Ed. You were close to Tyler. Hannah said you took him under your wing and mentored him. You knew exactly when he stopped working here and you hid his name from me for a reason. Why didn't you want us to know he was working here at the time?"

Ed still hesitated. "I wasn't hiding it, Tucker. It was just an innocent mistake. Even according to this printout you have, he was only here a few more weeks. It's been twenty years. It's difficult to remember back that far."

"Then you should have added him and let me verify it."

Ed shrugged like it wasn't a big deal but Tucker always trusted his gut and his gut was telling him that Ed was lying. This had been no mistake. He'd intentionally kept that name from them for some reason.

He glanced at the Bible verse painted on the barn wall outside Ed's office. *Proverbs 10:12: Hatred stirreth up strifes: but love covereth all sins*. He'd heard that Ed took pride in his faith and his belief in God. Caleb believed he was a man who could be trusted and so did Luke. And they both knew Ed better than Tucker did, at least the man Ed was today.

Why, then, was he trying to cover something up about a murder? That didn't make any sense.

He didn't have the same connection to Ed

that his cousins did, so he wasn't worried about hurting the man's feelings or straining their relationship. He turned to him and locked eyes with him. "I'm going to find the answers to this, Ed, and if I discover that you're hiding something or covering something up in this case, I'll make sure that you pay."

Caleb, Luke and even Brett had shared with him that Chet had found Jesus before he died and that was because of Ed's prompting. Ed had been working for the ranch for as long as Tucker could remember. He remembered him from when Tucker was a child and Tucker would help him with the horses. That was a good memory he had and he didn't want to think anything bad about Ed.

But facts didn't lie and Tucker's gut instincts hardly ever led him astray.

But he had a difficult time believing that Ed would ever do anything to harm his loyal friend and employer, Chet. Ed was one person Tucker was certain his grandfather would have risked covering up for.

He grimaced as he realized he was going in circles with this case. But he couldn't give up. He'd meant it when he'd told Grey that Ally deserved to know what had happened to her mother.

He wasn't giving up until he found her those answers.

* * *

Ally had asked her friend Jenny to remain with her while she waited for Tucker to arrive to pick her up from school. He'd texted he was on his way, so they waited for him on a bench outside the front entrance.

"So things must be getting serious with you and Tucker," Jenny commented.

"Why do you say that?"

She nudged Ally with her shoulder. "Only the way your face lights up when you're talking about him and the way you smile when reading his text messages."

Ally's face warmed and she was certain she was blushing.

"You like him, Ally. There's nothing wrong with that."

She'd always found Tucker attractive but something had changed between them after that kiss outside the shed and, for once, she wasn't going to fight it. She'd promised herself after the initial attraction to him that nothing could ever happen between them. After all, it was his grandfather, his kin, that had hidden the truth about her mother all of these years.

He pulled his truck to the curb, and Jenny nudged her again and flashed her a sly smile. "Take a risk, Ally. He's cute."

She waved goodbye to her friend then climbed into Tucker's pickup and buckled in.

"Sorry I ran a little late. My cousin just texted me. He wants me to swing by the police station. Want me to take you home first? It shouldn't take long."

"No, that's fine. I'll go with you." Given the choice, she would prefer to remain by his side. Her face warmed again as she realized her desire to stay close to him had more to do with her growing feelings for Tucker than her worry about being alone.

He drove to the police station and they both got out.

"I'm glad you made it," Caleb said as they walked in. He pointed down a hallway. "There's a break room down that way if you want to wait in there, Ally."

She nodded, then headed down the hall.

"I won't be long," Tucker called after her.

She walked into the break room and poured herself a cup of coffee. She tried not to focus on her feelings but Jenny had pushed open a door she'd struggled to keep closed when it came to Tucker. She couldn't deny it any longer. She more than liked him. If she was honest with herself, she was falling in love with Tucker.

She was overcome with the urge to tell him

and discover if he felt the same, but her cell phone rang before she could act on it.

She glanced at the screen. Abby.

"Hi, Abby."

"I'm glad I caught you," the other woman said. "I talked with my former producer at the TV station there in Jessup and he wants to send someone over to interview you about your mother's case. He's excited to cover a cold case from Jessup."

Her heart soared at this new development. "That's wonderful news." Finally, her mother's case was going to get the coverage it deserved.

"I'm texting you with a day and time. He'll send a reporter along with a camera crew to film the segment."

"Thank you for arranging this, Abby. I appreciate it so much."

"I was happy to help," she said, then ended the call.

Ally checked her texts and saw the interview information pop up on her screen. She couldn't wait to share this news with Tucker. He would be thrilled as well.

She tossed her coffee cup into the trash, then hurried into the bullpen. She could see Tucker and his cousins talking in the conference room and she rushed to the door to open it. She stopped before she did. They all looked deep in conversation and the furrows on Tucker's brow told her they were having a serious discussion that she probably shouldn't interrupt. Her news could wait until they were done with whatever they were discussing. Tucker still hadn't shared with her what was so important that his two cousins needed to come to town unexpectedly and stay while their wives returned home. She hadn't pressed him, either. If it had had something to do with her mother's case, Ally was certain he would have shared it with her.

She turned to head back to the break room, but stopped when she overheard a snippet of their conversation. Something about their grandfather, and she swore she heard the word *murder.* She turned around. If they believed their grandfather was involved in her mother's murder, she deserved to be included in the conversation.

She approached the conference room again and spotted writing on the whiteboard. On the top of the whiteboard were the words *Chet Harmon Murder Investigation.*

Ally's mind couldn't focus on that. Confusion flooded her. Were they saying that Chet had been murdered, too?

Anger and indignation slammed into her. They weren't meeting to discuss her mom's case. The cousins were meeting to investigate the murder of their grandfather.

And Tucker was with them.

Investigating his grandfather's death...and not her mom's.

Tucker must have sensed her glare because he turned to look at her.

Ally turned, too, and marched out of the police station.

She'd trusted Tucker to help her find the answers to her mother's disappearance but he'd only helped her because he'd been trying to find out who'd murdered his grandfather.

TEN

Tears filled Ally's eyes as she walked out of the police station and down the street. She felt like a fool. She'd initially been uneasy about trusting anyone in the Harmon family and it seems she'd been right. She'd thought Tucker had been on her side, but had he only been helping her in order to get answers about his grandfather's murder? She didn't even know if the two cases were connected in any way, however, the fact that he hadn't mentioned he and his cousins were investigating Chet's death meant he'd been keeping secrets from her.

She'd trusted him and he's betrayed her.

And, given that Luke and Brett had remained in town, they were obviously more concerned about their grandfather's investigation than her mother's. As she'd seen, the Harmon family took top priority.

She'd made her way through town before she realized she didn't have a ride home. She would need to call a cab. She took out her cell phone to make the call when suddenly Tucker's pickup pulled up at the curb.

He spoke to her through the open window. "Ally, what are you doing?"

She forced herself not to break down in front of him. "I'm going home."

"What's the matter? Why are you so mad?"

"I saw what you were doing, Tucker. I saw the whiteboard in the conference room and heard you all talking. You and your cousins are more worried about your grandfather's death than my mom's. You've been lying to me all this time." Once again, the Harmon family had looked after themselves.

"It's not like that," Tucker insisted.

"You've been investigating Chet's murder."

"Yes, but only because it might be in connection with your mother's disappearance."

She shook her head. "And suddenly, all of your cousins are working on my mother's case? This has more to do with him than with my mother. As usual, the Harmon family get what they want at the expense of everyone else."

She'd wondered why Tucker would take her side against his family to help her. Now, she knew the answer. He hadn't been helping her. He'd been looking for answers to his own for his grandfather's death.

She turned away from him. She couldn't even look at him. She'd stuck out her neck trusting him, only to be hurt. "Forget it, Tucker. I'm going home."

He got out of the truck. "Ally, you're placing yourself in unnecessary danger. Now, get in the pickup and I'll take you home."

She stopped walking, realizing that he was right. Plus, she didn't have a way home. She had a target on her back. And, after this betrayal, he at least owed her a ride home.

She gave a frustrated sigh then turned and headed for the truck. "Fine. Take me home." She climbed inside and slammed the door.

Tucker slid behind the wheel and started the engine. The ride to her house was silent as she fumed, holding on to her anger at him. It was the only way she could hold back the tears that threatened her. She couldn't wait to get home and let them flow.

He pulled into her driveway and she immediately reached for the door handle before he'd even completely stopped.

Tucker reached for her arm to stop her. "Ally, you have to believe I didn't do anything. I only just found out about my grandfather's murder. Caleb told us all yesterday."

"It doesn't matter because that's when my mother's case became important, isn't it? That's when the Harmon family decided she was worth finding."

"This is a good thing. Having others help this investigation is good."

He was right about that but it didn't make this situation any easier. "I know it is, Tucker, and I'm thankful that at least others have finally decided my mother's case needs to be investigated. But it should have been done ages ago. Why wasn't she important enough twenty years ago to find the answers? Her case has languished for decades. But Chet Harmon's case gets investigated right away and it's all hands on deck to help find his killer. It's not fair."

"I agree it's not fair but I've done everything I can to help you."

She jumped from the truck and hurried toward her front door, readying the key for the lock. Hot tears burned her eyes. She felt ready to explode with hurt and anger. Maybe it wasn't right, but it was the way she felt. Her mother had worked for Chet Harmon for years and her reward was to be murdered and hidden away, and her death had been covered up.

Tucker followed her up the walk. "Ally. Please don't push me away. You have to believe I've been on your side from the moment I met you. I'm still on your side. Can't you see how much I care about you?"

His words broke her, but she couldn't push past her anger. She'd been wishing for just this thing less than an hour before. But everything was different now. She shook her head. She couldn't even look at him. She bit back her weakness and put on a strong face as she turned to face him. "How could you think I could ever be with someone with the name Harmon? Your family is the reason I had to live my life without my mom. Your family prevented me from getting the answers I sought. Even now, your family is stonewalling me in my search for my mother. I could never be with you, Tucker. I could never love anyone who bore the name Harmon."

Her words had gutted him. She saw it in his expression, although he did his best to hide it. Her accusations had struck him just as she'd meant them to.

He nodded, but didn't speak for several moments. When he did, his voice cracked with pain. "I can't change the way I feel for you, Ally, and I don't want to. This isn't the end of us. I'm not giving up on you. On us." He slipped on his cowboy hat as he turned and walked back to his pickup.

She closed the front door and locked it, but watched as he climbed in his truck, started the engine and pulled away.

Only then did she let the tears loose. Only then did she allow herself to cry for her loss.

Tucker pulled into the parking lot at the police station and cut the engine. He'd gotten up early and followed discreetly behind Ally as she drove to work this morning. And he would be there when she got off to make sure she made it home safely.

His feelings after their blowup yesterday hadn't changed. He'd meant what he'd told her. He wasn't giving up on her. She might be mad at him, but he wasn't going to leave her unprotected.

He headed inside and found his cousins in the conference room, where they'd set up a command center for the investigation.

"How was Ally this morning?" Caleb asked him.

"She made it to school safely," Tucker told him. He hadn't told them what had transpired between them, but they'd all seen the way she'd stormed out of there yesterday, so he figured they could guess.

"I've ordered extra patrols around the school and her house," Caleb told him.

Tucker thanked him, then addressed all of his cousins. "Have we found anything useful?"

Brett pulled out his laptop. "I've been going

through the video surveillance feeds from the ranch. On the day Ally was attacked in the barn, I found five visitors." He pulled up the first image and Caleb shook his head.

"That's Jeb Morrison. He comes by every few weeks and Hannah gives him and his wife some vegetables from the garden. His wife has been battling cancer and he's had some heart issues, so she likes to help them out."

Morrison looked to be sixty-five or seventy, slim and sickly-looking. He would have been old enough to be around when Tonya went missing, however, he didn't look strong or healthy enough to be behind the attacks against Ally. Tucker had learned to never underestimate anyone, but he doubted Morrison was responsible.

Brett confirmed it with his next words. "The video doesn't show he went anywhere near the barn, either."

That was enough for Tucker. "Who else?"

"The veterinarian."

Tucker shook his head. "I interviewed him. He wasn't even in the state twenty years ago when Tonya went missing. Plus, one of the ranch hands was with him at the time Ally was attacked in the barn."

Brett nodded. "There was the delivery driver and his assistant from the feedstore."

"He'd gone out of town when I went to interview him. That struck me as suspicious." A family emergency could be an excuse for getting out of town before anyone realized he was involved.

"I didn't see him leave the truck at any time, but they were parked close to the barn."

So that meant he couldn't be ruled out until they had a chance to speak with him or someone else could be identified.

"This was the final visitor. He was also there during the time Ally was attacked." He pulled up an image that Tucker recognized right away.

"I know him."

Caleb glanced at the screen. "He doesn't look familiar. Who is he?"

"Tyler Grey. He used to work as a ranch hand here around the same time that Tonya went missing. I spoke with him. Both he and Ed claimed he hasn't been at Harmon Ranch in years."

Luke stood and grabbed his computer. "I know that name." He pulled up a file on his laptop. "I went through Grandpa Chet's phone records and he called a number registered to Tyler Grey three times the week he died, including just a few hours before."

That was all the evidence Tucker needed to know that Tyler Grey was involved in this.

Caleb rubbed the back of his neck and Tucker

could see it upset him to think Ed was involved. "We need to bring this Tyler Grey in for questioning. Then we'll need to talk to Ed, too, about why he's lying to us."

Luke rubbed his chin. "Why would Ed cover for this Tyler Grey?"

Tucker could see it was affecting them all. "I don't know, but we need to find out. Caleb, why don't you and I go and find him?"

Caleb nodded then pulled up Grey's information and sent it to his cell phone. Tucker knew the address of the office where he worked, but hadn't been to his home address.

They drove to the address listed as his residence and they got out. No one appeared to be at home when they rang the doorbell. The garage door was down and they heard no movement from inside. No one was home.

"Let's try his office," Caleb said, but when they arrived, no one there had seen him, either.

"He was supposed to be in the office this morning, but he hasn't shown up and he's not answering his cell phone," the receptionist told them. "It's not like him."

"We went by his house and no one was there, either. Do you know his wife?"

"No, his wife passed away a few years ago. She had heart problems. And they never had any kids."

Tucker flashed Caleb a look. That drug Grandpa Chet had been poisoned with had been something used for heart conditions. Coincidence? He didn't believe it. The evidence seemed to be digging Tyler Grey into a bigger hole.

Tucker wrote down his cell phone number and handed it to her. "If you see or hear from him, please call me."

They left the office and Caleb pulled out his cell phone and called the dispatcher. "I need to issue a BOLO for Tyler Grey. He's wanted for questioning in the murders of Chet Harmon and Tonya Fulton, and the attacks on Ally Fulton."

Once that was done, they checked out several of the construction sites the receptionist had given them, but found no signs of Grey anywhere. Most of the sites had been shut down for the day when Grey hadn't shown up.

Tucker glanced at the time. They'd spent all afternoon searching and it was nearly time for Ally to leave the school. With Grey's location unaccounted for, Tucker didn't want to leave her unprotected.

"Let's ride by the school," he told his cousin. "I want to update Ally about Tyler Grey and make sure she makes it home."

Caleb nodded. "I'll stop and get out at the police station and you can take my truck."

Tucker was fine with that since they had time before school let out. He was hoping Ally would listen to him. He'd tried to call her and text her, but she hadn't returned any of his messages. He understood she was mad, but she had to think about her safety, too.

Caleb pulled to the curb by the police station, then hopped out so Tucker could slide behind the wheel. "I'll let you know if we get a hit on that BOLO," he said before Tucker sped away.

He pulled into the school's parking lot as Ally was walking from the entrance with her friend. The moment she spotted him, her demeanor changed. She tensed and hurried to her rental car.

Tucker pulled in beside her car and hopped out. "Ally, I need to speak with you."

"Tucker, I told you I didn't want to see you."

"I know, but we have new information." He pulled out his cell phone and pulled up the image of Tyler Grey from the ranch's video feeds. "Do you recognize this man? Have you seen him around?"

She glanced at the phone, then shook her head. "I don't know him. Who is he?"

"His name is Tyler Grey. We're looking for him to question him about the attack against you in the barn. Brett discovered he was at the ranch at the time you were attacked. When I interviewed him, he told me he hadn't been there in years."

She frowned and worry crept into her face. "So you think this guy was the one who's been attacking me?"

"Why else would he lie?" There might be a logical reason for it, but anytime someone lied to the police about their actions, it shot up a red flag for Tucker. "We've put out a BOLO on him but he's nowhere to be found. We're checking out his house, his business and multiple construction sites his company is working on around town."

"Did he know my mom?"

"Possibly. That's another red flag. He and Ed both claimed he wasn't working there at the time she vanished, but we've found payroll records that refute that."

"So this could be the man who killed her?"

He didn't want to get her hopes up until they knew for certain, but he wasn't holding anything back from her again. "Possibly."

She seemed to absorb that information for a moment. Her chin quivered but she took a deep breath and steadied herself. "I appreciate you letting me know, Tucker. I'll be on the lookout for him."

She started for her car and opened the door. He shut it. "Ally, this man could be dangerous.

I can't ensure your safety if you won't even let me around you."

"I want to trust you, Tucker. I really do. I put all my trust in you and I got hurt. Every time I see you, I'm reminded of that pain. I need some time to get past the fact that you hid your grandfather's investigation from me. I pray you do find this man. I want him to pay for what he did to my mom, for what he took from me."

She pulled open her car door and got inside. He watched her drive away, still angry at him. He didn't like seeing her like this, and the only thing he wanted more than catching this guy and ending the threat against her…was her.

He climbed into Caleb's SUV and followed behind her as she headed home, maintaining a safe distance. He slowed to watch as she pulled into her driveway and parked in the garage, breathing a sigh of relief that, at least, she was safe at home.

He'd arranged with Caleb to have patrol officers driving by her house frequently. He hoped it was enough. He couldn't force her to accept his protection, but she couldn't stop him from caring about her, either.

Ally pulled into her garage and hit the button to lower the garage door. It rumbled as it closed. She didn't get out right away, but instead leaned against the steering wheel. The past two days had been extremely stressful. Tucker had continued to text and try to call her, but she'd refused to talk to him until he'd cornered her in the parking lot. He'd hurt her too badly to forgive him that easily for his betrayal.

She was thankful she'd insisted on having a rental car, or else she would have had no way to get back and forth to work.

God, please help me overcome my anger.

She didn't want to be angry anymore, but she wasn't sure how to overcome her feelings. Finally, she decided she couldn't keep spinning her wheels. Despite how she'd pushed him away, he was still actively working to keep her safe and to solve her mother's case. That had to account for something. Yes, he'd made a mistake but maybe—*maybe*—she'd overreacted.

She was going to call Tucker and try to figure out how to get past it. If finding his grandfather's killer was what it took to find her mother's murderer, she supposed it was worth it.

She only wished he'd told her from the beginning.

She grabbed her purse and bag from the passenger's seat, and opened the car door. She got out and, before she could even close her car door, someone grabbed her from behind, pressing his hand over her mouth.

Her purse and bags fell as she tried to push him away, but her assailant's other hand pinned her arms. He shoved her back into the car and pushed her across to the passenger's seat before hopping in and starting the ignition. Ally spun around to fight back, but he punched her in the face. Pain stung her cheek and she grabbed the spot and pressed against it. She turned back to him only to see he'd pulled a knife and pointed it at her.

"That's enough," he hissed.

She felt anger and rage flowing off him and his hot, heavy breath fell upon her. She glanced up into his face and saw the identity of her attacker.

Tyler Grey. The former ranch hand at Harmon Ranch. Tucker had shown her his photo less than an hour ago. She hadn't recognized him them but seeing him now face-to-face brought back a rush of memories of the day her mother died. She was staring into the face of the man who'd stabbed her mom. The man who'd raped then later murdered her mother. And who might even be her own father.

He hit the button to raise the garage door. "Get down on the floor," he commanded her, waving the knife.

She reluctantly did so. "Why are you doing this?"

He ignored her question and adjusted the rearview mirror, then backed out.

Her heart was racing as he drove. This wasn't good. If he'd grabbed her, his intentions weren't good. She wished she had some way to alert Tucker that she was in trouble, then shamefully realized she'd pushed him away so hard that he wouldn't even be looking for her. He wouldn't know she was in trouble until it was too late for her.

Tyler Grey was cleaning up. He'd assaulted then murdered her mother, killed Chet Harmon to keep him from exposing him and targeted her practically since the moment she'd started digging for answers.

Now, he was going to kill her, too, in order to cover up his crimes.

"Why are you doing this?" she asked him again. If she was going to die, she wanted to know why. She wanted an explanation.

Still, he ignored her demands.

"Why are you doing this?" she repeated, this time loudly. "Tell me or I'll scream for help." She wasn't sure who would or could hear her, but she wasn't going down without a fight.

His jaw clenched and he jerked the car. She heard gravel and knew he'd pulled the car to the shoulder. He grabbed her and punched her, sending stinging ripples through her face. She gasped at the pain and groaned. He pulled a bandanna from his pocket and shoved it into her mouth. "Now, shut up," he demanded.

He yanked her from her car and shoved her toward a red truck, opening the passenger door and pushing her inside. He took a pair of zip ties from his pocket and bound her hands. Then he shoved her to the floor, climbed inside, pulled the pickup onto the road and sped away.

The reality of what was happening settled inside of her. Grey had her now and he was going to do whatever it took to keep her from exposing his secret life.

Tucker headed back to the police station to meet up with his cousins and figure out a plan to locate Tyler Grey. They would have to talk to Ed, too, about his lies, and that would be difficult for everyone, especially Caleb.

His cell phone rang. He glanced at the screen. Caleb.

"Hey, Caleb, what's happening?"

"We just received a call in Dispatch from Ally's neighbor. Her garage door is standing open and she said it looks like there's been a struggle."

Tucker spun the truck around, his gut clenching at the thought of something happening to her after his drive-by. "I was just there. I'm heading back that way."

"I have a patrol unit en route, but you're closer."

"I'll let you know what I find."

He turned his truck into the neighborhood where Ally lived, slowing as he approached her house. Instantly, he knew something was wrong. The garage door was open but her car was gone. That struck him as odd. She always kept that door closed. He parked by the curb and got out. As he walked up the driveway, he noticed her purse and bag lying on the garage floor. Her purse was lying close to the sensor and its items strewn about. It had probably kept the garage from completely closing, which might have been a break for them. If it had closed, her neighbor wouldn't have noticed and called, and no one would have been aware Ally was in danger.

He kneeled down and picked up her wallet. It still held her ID, credit cards and cash. Whatever had happened here hadn't been a robbery, but someone had obviously surprised her enough that she'd dropped her purse and scattered the contents.

With her car missing, he doubted she was in the house, but he had to check it out. He opened the door and called out to her, praying he would hear a response. Nothing. He walked through the house, clearing each room one by one. She wasn't here. Someone had grabbed her probably as she got out of her car in the garage. Perhaps he'd sneaked in before the door tried to close because he knew she was diligent about closing it behind her. It was a safety concern for her. The fact that it was still open made it clear that something bad had happened to her.

He pulled out his phone and called Caleb. Tucker would need help from the police in finding her. And he was going to find her. He couldn't let something terrible happen to Ally.

He couldn't lose her now that he'd fallen in love with her.

ELEVEN

Tucker was desperate to find Ally. And he was sure he knew who had taken her. Tyler Grey. He went back to the police station and met up with his cousins.

"He took her—he took her. He took Ally."

Caleb shook his head. "We don't know that for certain but he's our main suspect until we find out differently. If he knows we're onto him, he's more dangerous than ever."

Luke put his hand on Tucker's shoulder. "Don't worry. We'll find her."

That wasn't good enough. He needed answers. They knew who took Ally. Now, they just had to find him.

"I updated the BOLO on Grey," Caleb said. "We still haven't had any hits on it."

"Has anyone tried his office again?" Luke asked.

"I called over there but they said they still haven't seen or heard from him," Caleb responded. "I've got a warrant to get in front of a judge to try to get access to his phone's location data. Maybe we can find him that way."

Tucker was sure that would take hours. They needed to find him now before he harmed Ally. Time was not on her side now that she was in Grey's hands. He couldn't stand the thought of her being in danger and him unable to help her.

He turned to his cousin. "We know one person who can find Grey."

Caleb's eyes darkened and he leaned against the desk, his face weary and troubled. But he finally nodded. He opened his desk drawer and pulled out his gun, slipping it into the holster. "Let's go question him."

Tucker rode with Caleb in his SUV as Brett and Luke followed behind them. Tucker could see Caleb was tense as they headed toward the ranch. "I'm sorry about this," Tucker told him. He hadn't been looking to cause his cousin pain.

Caleb shook his head, but his grip on the steering wheel didn't ease. "This is not your doing, Tucker. You're right. Ed has the answers and we need them. Whatever he's hiding, for whatever reason he's doing this, we have to know. I just have a difficult time believing he would let an innocent woman get hurt. That's not the Ed I know."

They arrived at the ranch and pulled up at the barn, then got out and headed inside, looking for Ed. It was time for answers. Whatever he was holding back he was going to give up today. Tucker was determined to do whatever it took to find Ally and he didn't have the same loyalty to Ed that Caleb and the others did.

Ed was at his desk in his office inside the barn when they arrived. He looked surprised to see all four of them together when they stepped inside. He didn't stand, but just gave them a quizzical look. "What's going on?"

Tucker stepped forward and took the lead. This wasn't the time to hold back. "Tyler Grey has abducted Ally."

Ed's face paled and he dropped the pen in his hand. He rubbed his face. "Oh, no."

Tucker approached him. "I don't know why you're protecting him, Ed, but you have to help us find him. Ally's life is in danger."

He kept his head down and didn't look at any of them. Tucker didn't think that he was going to respond to help them. Anger burned through him. Ally's life was in danger and Ed was still covering for a killer.

Caleb must have noticed Tucker about to lose his cool because he put a calming hand on his shoulder, then moved past him and kneeled beside the chair, where Ed remained sitting.

"Her life is in danger, Ed. Why are you protecting this man? You are better than this. I've known you for a long time and I know that you would never let harm come to an innocent woman."

But he already had with Tonya.

Tucker continued to press him. "I know you hid the fact that he worked here when Ally's mom vanished. You have to know that he is involved. He assaulted Tonya Fulton, then killed her, too. Now, he's killed Grandpa Chet and abducted Ally. Why would you ever cover for a man like that?"

Ed moved his hands away from his face but his color had not returned. He looked beaten down and forlorn, but his resigned expression told Tucker he was about to come clean. That was a step in the right direction. If he didn't, Tucker didn't know what he might do.

"I've always had a soft spot for that kid," Ed told them. "I knew it when he came here. I always tried to help him even though I knew he was probably involved."

Caleb shook his head. "I don't understand it. Why would you help a man like that? Why would you continue to help him all these years even knowing what he what he did?"

Pain filled Ed's face as he revealed the truth. "Because he's my son."

Caleb took a few steps back, a strained expression on his face. "I—I didn't know you had a son."

"Neither did I. He was sixteen when he showed up at the ranch. His mother was a woman I'd dated briefly in my younger days. She never told me about him. Of course, I never married, so the idea of having a son at that time in my life was amazing. I didn't tell anyone except Chet. He knew. I didn't want people to think that Tyler was getting special favor just because he was the ranch manager's son. I had this twisted idea that he needed to work for what he got. When I called his mom to find out more about him, she alerted me that he'd been in all kinds of trouble—lying, stealing, burglary and assault. She was relieved when he took off. I blamed myself for not being there for him. I thought I could change him, reform him. At the very least, I could help him get his life together."

Luke folded his arm. "And when you learned he'd assaulted a woman? How did you justify covering for him then?"

"I did not know about that for many years," he told them all. "Tonya could never identify her attacker and I had no reason to suspect my son. It wasn't until a few weeks before she went missing that I began to suspect something was wrong.

"I noticed her watching Tyler. One day, I saw her following him. She retrieved a cigarette of his off the ground and put it in a plastic bag. I couldn't help but wonder what she was doing so I asked her. She told me she suspected Tyler was the man who had assaulted her all those years earlier. She wanted to get his DNA to perform a paternity test on her daughter. If it came back that he was Ally's father, she would know he was the man who attacked her. I questioned her about why she believed Tyler was the man who had attacked her. She said she recognized the tattoo on his neck. It was the only thing she'd been able to see clearly during the attack. That's when it occurred to me that he had been taking great pains to cover it up, but I just thought he was trying to be a good worker, respectful. She said she saw him one day with his shirt off working in the stable. That's when she knew it was him. I asked her to come to me with the results before she confronted him. She agreed, and when the results came back and showed him as Ally's father, I knew for sure what he'd done. She told me she was going to the police with the result and that the statute of limitations was almost up, so she had to go now. I begged her to wait. I begged her to give me the opportunity to confront him first with what he'd done, and maybe I could get a confession out of him. I still wanted to save him. I thought if he confessed and turned himself in, he could make things right. I guess she trusted me because she agreed to wait. Only, when I confronted him with the terrible thing that he'd done, he continued to deny it. I tried to tell him that DNA doesn't lie and that she had a paternity test showing that he was the father of that little girl. He insisted he would take care of it. He insisted he was going to turn himself in. God help me, I believed him."

Caleb nodded. "You wanted to believe him."

"So then when Tonya went missing, I immediately confronted him and he insisted he hadn't done anything. What with her accusations of rape against him, he knew he would be a suspect in her disappearance. He said he'd had nothing to do with her disappearance. He made me feel so guilty for not believing in him. I still felt so guilty about not being there for him when he was growing up, so I went to Chet and asked him for help. I didn't tell him about the assault accusation because I knew what he would think. I assured him that Tyler wasn't involved and he took me at my word. He used his influence to help me protect my son. He did it because I'd been a loyal employee for years, and a friend. Tonya had also been a loyal employee. I believe that's the reason he felt compelled to provide for Ally all those years."

"Then what happened?" Tucker demanded. Something must have happened to cause Tyler to target Chet.

"I was a different man then. It was years later that I found the Lord and changed my sinful ways. I struggled with this secret, but it had been so long by that time and I still had nothing but my doubts about Tyler. As you know, your grandfather found the Lord, too, just a year or so before he died. I think he must have had the same struggle about the cover-up. A few weeks before he died, Chet came to me and told me that Tonya's daughter had been trying to contact him. That she was trying to find out what happened to her mom. He said he wasn't going to cover for Tyler any longer. He was going to tell her daughter everything that had happened. He said he owed me, but he owed Tonya something, too, and he couldn't cover up for Tyler any longer. I assured Chet that I understood, and I did. Neither of us should ever have been involved with that and it was the right thing to come clean. So I called Tyler and told him that Chet was going to contact him and why. It was only a few days after that that Chet died. Of course, I wondered if he'd done something to Chet—the timing just seemed too coincidental—but then the autopsy came back showing he'd died of natural causes. I didn't think anything more about it. I figured Tyler couldn't have caused Chet's death."

"Yet, you still didn't come clean about what Tyler had done to Tonya, did you?"

He shook his head. "No, I didn't."

Caleb sighed. "You could have come to me with this, Ed. You should have."

"I know. I know what I've done."

"And when the attacks against Ally started? What did you think then?" Tucker demanded.

Ed glanced up at him. "I didn't want to think he was involved."

"Yet you kept the employment records from Tucker when he asked so you must have suspected something," Luke said.

Tucker smoothed his hair back as frustration and fear fought for control of him. Now that they knew the truth about how this had come about, it didn't change the fact that Ally was now the one at the mercy of a killer. Tucker leaned across the desk and confronted him directly. "You can't cover for him any longer, Ed. He's taken Ally and he's going to kill her. We have to find him. Now." He picked up the cell phone from the desk and handed it to Ed. "Call him. He's not answering for us or his employees, but he might answer for you. Keep calling until he does. Don't let him know we're onto him. Find out where he's at right now. Find out where he's taken Ally."

Reluctantly, Ed took the phone and gave a resigned nod.

"Wait," Luke said. "I have a tracking device in the back of my SUV." He hurried to his vehicle and returned with a device that he hooked up to Ed's phone. They could use it to track Tyler's position as long as Ed could keep him on the phone long enough. It was a better plan than simply relying on Ed to convince his son to give himself up and release Ally unharmed.

After all, Tyler Grey had everything to lose, which placed Ally in a precarious position.

Reluctantly, Ed dialed his son's number. He didn't answer.

"Try him again," Tucker insisted. "Keep trying until he picks up. And keep it on speaker so we can hear the conversation."

After four tries, Tyler finally answered.

"What do you want?" he demanded without even uttering any pleasantries to his own father.

"Tyler, what have you done? Did you kidnap that woman?"

Tucker grimaced. Ed wasn't staying on script. He wasn't supposed to be telling Grey that they were onto him.

He responded angrily. "I haven't abducted

anyone. You're always quick to blame me for something."

Ed leaned on his elbows and brushed his hand against his forehead. "Tyler, son, the woman who is in town to find her mother. She's been attacked several times. Tell me you didn't have anything to do with that."

"You always accuse me, Ed."

"So you weren't involved then?"

"I didn't do anything wrong, but I won't allow this woman to ruin my life. I have a thriving business and a reputation to maintain. I won't let her ruin that with all of these accusations about something that happened forever ago."

"If you haven't done anything, then there's nothing to worry about."

Tucker was listening intently, trying to pinpoint any words or background noises that might clue them in to his location. He glanced over Luke's shoulder at the tap and trace on the laptop. It was zeroing in on Tyler's location, but it still hadn't pinpointed it yet. Ed needed to keep him on the phone.

Tucker urged him on with a keep-him-talking hand gesture.

"There's something else," Ed continued. "Caleb just told me. They're changing Chet's manner of death from natural causes to homicide. They said he was poisoned."

Grey spouted out a string of expletives. "And what did you say?"

"I didn't say a word, Tyler."

"Good. You'd better not." The threatening tone in the younger man's voice was unmistakable even through the phone. It was obvious that he was used to bullying people to get his own way.

"Ty, did you have something to do with Chet's death?"

"Just keep your mouth shut, Ed." With that, he abruptly ended the call.

Tucker leaned over Luke's shoulder. "Did you get it?"

"Partially. His phone was pinging off a tower on the outskirts of town, but he didn't stay on long enough to get an accurate location."

Tucker rubbed the back of his neck. At least they had a general idea. If he had to stick his head out of the window and shout Ally's name, he would do so.

Ed glanced at the laptop screen. "I know where he's at," Ed volunteered. "He's working on a building out that way right on the edge of town. Right now, it's just a construction site."

Tucker wasn't familiar with the area—the construction site where he'd interviewed Grey had been on the opposite side of town—but Ed gave Caleb directions and he seemed to know exactly where he was talking about.

"I know where that is," Caleb told them. "Let's go." He stopped and turned back to Ed. "You're going to have to come back to the police station with me, Ed."

"What for? I've been cooperative."

"You covered up at least one murder." Tucker could see something else playing on his grim expression. He finally realized what it was. Betrayal. "Plus, I need to make sure you don't call Tyler back and warn him we're onto him."

Ed's face reddened but he nodded and stood. Tucker hated for Caleb's sake that he'd been betrayed by someone he'd trusted. Caleb and Luke both had a close relationship with Ed. Caleb had lived on the ranch since he was twelve and interacted with Ed on a daily basis. Luke and his family had also lived on the ranch and grown close to the manager. Tucker didn't know how close Brett was to him, but Tucker didn't have the same emotional attachment to him as the others did. He had fond memories of Ed from when he was a child, but they had only been on friendly terms since Tucker had returned to Harmon Ranch.

The tension in the vehicle was high as they drove back to the station. After arriving, Caleb had Ed set up in a holding room while Tucker,

Luke, Brett and several of Caleb's SWAT officers geared up. Grey may not know they were coming, but he was still dangerous and they had to be prepared.

As the swirl of activity happened around him, Tucker stopped and took a long, deep breath. His heart was racing and fear was seeping into him. He had to compose himself. He needed to be at his sharpest if he had any hope of rescuing Ally from a madman.

He lowered his head and whispered a prayer that he wasn't already too late.

"Ready?" Caleb asked.

Tucker looked up to see his cousin in his tactical gear. Tucker nodded and picked up his own equipment bag. "Ready." This was far from his first tactical situation. He'd cared about each one of them. Each time he'd donned this uniforms, someone's life was in jeopardy. However, this was the first time he'd had a personal stake in the outcome.

Ally's voice was sore from screaming for help. Tyler had driven to a construction site and shoved her into a deep hole. She'd tried everything to escape, but the dirt walls kept giving as she tried climbing to the top. The loose dirt caused her to slip and fall back to the bottom. Even if her hands hadn't been tied together, she doubted she could have made it to the top. Her screams for help seemed to evaporate on the wind. No one was coming to help her. She hadn't seen anyone around when Tyler had dragged her through the construction lot. If he owned this place, he could close it down and no one would be around to see or hear her cries for help.

Her mind was whirling trying to come up with some way out of this. If she didn't, she was going to die in this hole. For all she knew, Tyler had left her here to die. If he hadn't, he would soon return to finish her off.

Either way, she was in trouble.

Ally looked around for something, anything, to help her out of this mess. A wave of fear washed over her. She was going to die in this hole and never have the opportunity to apologize to Tucker. She sat down and leaned against the back of the dirt wall. There was no point in denying it any longer. She'd overreacted and pushed him away out of fear. The Harmon family might have had a hand in covering up her mother's disappearance, but Tucker had been a child, like her. He'd played no role and had been estranged from his grandfather for years. Plus, he'd done nothing but try to help her since the moment they'd met.

He was blameless when it came to her mother's case.

She put her hands over her face. She'd messed up. She could have had everything and if she hadn't pushed Tucker away, she might not be in this situation. He would have been with her, protecting her. She'd blown it again and everything was going wrong.

God, please don't let this be the end. She wanted another chance to tell Tucker how much she loved him and how she wished for a future with him. Her gut told her it wasn't meant to be. She wasn't going to make it out of this mess.

Suddenly, she heard movement above her.

She scrambled to her feet and glanced up, covering her eyes against the blaring sun, waiting and anxious to see who appeared. "Hello! Hello! Help me, please. I'm down here!" Hopefully, someone had realized she was missing and come to find her.

She held her breath as footsteps moved closer. Then a shadow appeared above her. The figure of a man.

She started to shout for help again, but stopped when Grey's face hovered above her. He kneeled down. "You can stop hollering," he told her. "No one can hear you. I've closed down this site. No one is anywhere for miles."

The smugness in his voice and demeanor angered her. She was still afraid, but she wasn't going down without a fight. If she was going to die, she at least wanted answers. "I know what you did to my mother, Tyler. I remember you. You killed her on the bank of the lake."

He didn't deny it. In fact, he seemed proud. "You should have died, too, that day, Ally. That was the plan, anyway. For you both to disappear. Then everyone would believe that she'd just run off."

She shuddered at the regret she heard in his voice for not killing her, too. "Why didn't you kill me that day?"

"You ran off. I tried to find you, but I couldn't very well leave your mother's body lying by the lake, could I? I had to hide it first. By the time I went looking for you, one of the other ranch hands had found you in the stalls and taken you to the main house. It was too late. I still did my best to float the story that your mom ran off with a man. Some people believed it."

His lies had managed to turn people against Ally's mom, but those who'd known her best had never believed it.

"Why did you do it, Tyler? Why did you kill my mother?" Tears pressed against her eyes, but she tried not to cry.

He gave a weary sigh and shook his head, giving in. Either he was tired of listening to her, or maybe he thought he might as well unburden himself after all these years. After all, Ally wasn't going to be able to do anything with the information he shared with her.

"She threatened me. She tried to rope me into a rape charge, then said she was going to the police. I was just getting my life together. She had no right to try to set me up."

His words made her sick, mostly because Ally knew they were lies. She knew Tyler Grey was her biological father, which meant he had assaulted her mother. She hadn't been threatening to rope him into anything. He'd attacked her and she'd obviously finally been able to prove it with the paternity test.

"I couldn't let her go to the police so I had to stop her."

Hearing him admit that sent waves of pain and grief through her. It hit her harder than she'd expected. Knowing was one thing, but hearing him confess it was another.

She pushed back the sobs that threatened to overcome her. She couldn't focus on that now. She was finally getting the answers she wanted. He was talking, confessing to her, and crying wouldn't do anything but stop him from continuing this admission of guilt.

It didn't matter to him now because he knew she wasn't getting out of this. She had to keep him talking.

"Where's her body? What did you do to her?

Where is she? Please, I've waited for so long to know the truth. Where is she?"

He sighed and rubbed his face. She could see that he was getting irritated and just wanted her to shut up and die. "We were building a new machine shed at the ranch. I buried her under it."

The truth stabbed her through the heart. Her mother had never left Harmon Ranch. She'd been there all this time. Ally gasped, realizing that she and Tucker had taken shelter in that shed, unaware that her mother was buried beneath it.

"That's enough," he shouted, then walked away.

Ally leaned against the wall and slid down to a sitting position. She allowed the tears to flow for her mother. She finally knew the truth and now she was going to take that information with her to her own grave.

Tucker's muscles clenched as they neared the construction site. He readied his weapon and checked his earpiece so he could remain in communication with the rest of the team. This was a new team and he missed his old one. They'd trained together and knew the complexities of one another. But he didn't have time to get to know these guys. He was inserting himself into their unit out of necessity. It made him a little uncomfortable, but it wasn't going to keep him from being involved. Not with Ally's life hanging in the balance.

Besides, he trusted Caleb. And, by extension, his officers.

Caleb stopped the SUV but reached out to grab Tucker's arm before getting out. "My team is well trained but we don't have the experience you have dealing with situations like this. Do you feel comfortable to take lead? I know how personal this is for you."

"I'm fine. My only concern is finding Ally and getting her to safety. I can keep my emotions in check long enough to do that." He'd been trained to tamp down emotion and remain calm and collected during a confrontation, but his training hadn't prepared him for confronting the man who'd abducted the woman he loved.

Nothing could have prepared him for that.

Tucker got out and readied his gear. He took a deep breath. The fence surrounding the construction site was covered but he could see they had a lot of area to cover. Ally and Grey could be anywhere on this construction site.

"Here's a map of the site," Caleb said, rolling it out on the hood of the truck.

"Where did you get this?"

"I sent Hansen by Grey's office and had them give us a copy."

"How do you know they didn't call him to let him know we were coming?"

Caleb shook his head. "I don't, but he hasn't been responding to them all day, so I took a risk."

Tucker was thankful he'd made that call. At least now they knew what they were walking into. Tucker studied the schematic, then made a plan. He sent several officers to the east side of the property and some to the west, while he and Caleb and his cousins would head straight in. They needed to surround the site in case Grey tried to flee. He wasn't getting away this time.

Tucker raised his gun as Caleb cut the lock off the entrance gate. He led them inside. Caleb, Luke and Brett followed him in, along with several other officers from Caleb's force while the others scattered. Tucker scanned the area. No movement was apparent and he didn't hear any screams for help. That could mean Ally was tied up...or worse. He pushed away that thought. He couldn't let it linger in his mind if he hoped to do his job.

He swept the area. Nothing. There were several floors to the building under construction. They were going to have to search them all, as well as the entire construction site.

God, please keep her safe until I can reach her.

He couldn't even let himself wonder if she was still alive. He had to assume she was.

He and Luke checked the first floor while the others split up to spread out and search the rest of the building.

They cleared the entire building, but didn't find Ally and there was no sign of Grey.

He heard a rumbling and hurried out the front of the building, then circled around to the back. He spotted a cement truck, its agitator spinning. He bolted around to the cab and pulled open the door. The cab was empty. He kept running, circling the building, and spotted a figure standing at the back of the truck holding the chute and readying the concrete to pour into a hole.

Tucker stopped a moment before he realized what was happening. His eyes scanned the area and he spotted a hole in the ground and assumed the figure—Grey—was preparing to fill it in with concrete.

Ally!

He knew instinctively this wasn't a simple construction task. Grey was cleaning up after himself and trying to cover up his involvement. Making Ally disappear was part of his cleanup task.

She was in there.

He trained his gun on Grey. "Get away from the truck!"

Grey spun at the sound of his voice but didn't stop. He pressed the lever and Tucker heard the sound of the concrete releasing. Grey turned back and fired. Tucker fired back, hitting Grey in the leg. He fell to the ground. Tucker ran toward the truck and pushed the chute away as concrete started to spill out.

He glanced down the hole and spotted Ally at the bottom pressed up against the side. Grey had been going to drown her in concrete. That was diabolical.

"Tucker, watch out!" Caleb shouted.

Tucker spun and saw Grey raise his gun at him.

Tucker kicked it from his hand before he could fire. The gun went flying and Caleb and his cousins hurried over to help restrict Grey.

Brett ran over and turned off the concrete truck.

Caleb zip-tied Grey's hands then handed him off to another officer.

Tucker kneeled down and lifted the grate from the deep trench, then hopped inside. He took out his knife and cut the zip ties around Ally's hands and arms.

She fell into his embrace and he pulled her close to him. His heart was still racing from the close call. If they hadn't been able to find her, Grey would have encased her in concrete in a matter of minutes, burying her alive.

He kissed her and her arms encircled him.

"You found me," she whispered, her voice full of relief.

"Did you ever doubt it?"

She stared up at him. "I wasn't sure. After those terrible things I said to you…"

He shook his head. "Nothing you said was wrong, Ally, but that's not who I am. Nothing you could ever say would prevent me from coming to find you once I knew you were in danger."

"But how did you know?"

"A neighbor called in that your garage was standing open so I went by your house."

"You were checking up on me? Even after all the terrible things I said to you?"

He pulled his lips into a grin. "I couldn't leave you unprotected. I'm sorry I wasn't there when Grey grabbed you."

"That's not your fault, Tucker. It's mine. You've done nothing but try to help me. I'm so sorry. I'll never push you away again. Tucker, I don't ever want to be without you. I love you."

His heart swelled at her words and he pulled her to him for another kiss. "I love you, too, Ally. I never want to be without you, either. Will you marry me?"

She nodded and tears filled her eyes. "I'd love to marry you, Tucker Harmon."

He kissed her again.

Suddenly shadows appeared overhead. They both looked up to see his cousins standing over them, watching.

"Are you two planning on staying down there?" Brett asked them.

Tucker stared up at his cousins. "We're getting married," he told them.

They all grinned down at him. "That's great news," Caleb said. "Are you making this trench your new home or are you ready to climb out now?"

He stared down at Ally and stroked her face. He only wanted to be with her.

"Are you ready to get out of here?"

"Definitely."

Tucker helped Ally up and Caleb grabbed her arms and helped her up. Tucker followed. Once they were on solid ground, he checked on Grey, who was being loaded into the back of a police cruiser. Good. He was going to pay for all the pain and harm he'd done.

Then he put his arm around Ally and walked her to safety. "Let's get out of here," he whispered to her and she leaned into him.

He was ready to start their new life together.

EPILOGUE

Ally kneeled and placed flowers by the headstone that had just been installed at her mother's new grave site. Her remains had been found under the shed just as Tyler had told her he'd buried her there. She was grateful that Tucker and his cousins had made the decision to demolish the shed to honor Ally and her mom. She would never be able to look at that building without that terrible memory returning.

Ally had chosen a final resting place for her mom right here in Jessup, where her she'd lived and died. It also made it convenient for Ally to visit since she, too, had come to consider this town her home over the last year. She loved her job at the middle school and the kids she worked with, along with the friends she'd made since moving here. Most of all, she and Tucker had found one another here.

Tucker had chosen not to return to his job in Dallas, but to instead remain in Jessup and make Harmon Ranch his home. He'd assured her it hadn't been a difficult decision to make, either, once he knew his future included her. After all the suffering they'd endured, they'd both finally found a place to call home.

Ally reached for his hand as they walked back toward his pickup and he pulled her close. "I'm glad you finally have the peace you've been searching for," he told her as he kissed her.

"I'm glad she's here," Ally told him, referring to her mother. "I thought when I finally learned the truth that I would feel different, but it still hurts."

Tyler Grey was currently sitting in jail awaiting trial for her abduction and attempted murder, and the district attorney was looking at filing charges against him for her mom's murder as well as that of Chet Harmon. Tyler was finally going to pay for the evil things he'd done and that gave Ally a sense of relief.

Now was the time for her and Tucker to get on with their lives.

He drove them back to the ranch. As they passed the barn, she stiffened. Knowing that Chet and Ed had covered up her mother's rape and murder for all those years was painful. Ed had apologized to Ally for his actions and confessed to her how Chet had decided to come clean, too, before he was killed. Luke had dug into Chet's phone and bank records and discovered he'd met up with Tyler at the diner the day he'd died. They'd surmised—because Tyler was publicly denying everything—that he'd used that coffee chat to introduce the poison that ultimately killed Chet.

Ally was glad to know that Chet had planned to tell her the truth. Caleb was struggling to come to terms with Ed's involvement in all of this. He'd known Ed longer and been closer to him than any of them besides Hannah, who'd also been stunned by the revelation. Ed was also facing charges for his role in covering for his son and had made the decision to retire from Harmon Ranch for good. It was, she hoped, the end of secrets at Harmon Ranch.

Tucker bypassed the barn, but didn't drive all the way up to the farmhouse. He parked, then got out, pulling on Ally's arm to follow him.

"What are we doing?" she asked.

"I have a surprise for you." He led her to the corral and pointed out a horse getting used to her new surroundings.

He looked very pleased with himself but Ally was confused. "What am I looking at? The horse?"

He pushed up his hat. "Yep. Your horse. I bought her for you, Ally. So you can recapture your childhood. I don't want you to be afraid any longer. I want you to know that I'll always be here to protect you."

"Tucker, she's beautiful." She was overwhelmed with such a thoughtful gift. Her instinct was to push away and run, recalling that terrible day in the stables. She reached out and hesitantly stroked the horse, who pressed her nose against Ally's hand, and she instantly eased.

She laughed, then looked up at him. "Why did you buy me a horse?"

"If you're going to be a rancher, you need a horse."

She shook her head and stepped away from him. "Oh, no, Tucker. I'm a teacher, not a rancher. You're the one who's going to be the rancher."

He pulled her to him and she leaned against him. "As long as you promise to be the wife of a rancher, I'll be happy."

She smiled and just before their lips met again, made him the promise he longed to hear. "I can't wait to be the wife of a rancher."

* * * * *

Dear Reader,

Wrapping up a series is always bittersweet. I love the excitement of reaching the end of the stories, but I'm also sad to see the characters go. That's my feeling as I say goodbye to the Harmon cousins and the end of my Cowboy Protectors series.

I hope you enjoyed getting to know Tucker and Ally, and learning the truth about the murders that occurred at Harmon Ranch. I look forward to starting a new series, and meeting and getting to know new characters, new dangers and new romances. I hope you'll join me.

I love to hear from my readers! Please keep in touch. You can reach me online at my website www.virginiavaughanonline.com or follow me on Facebook at www.Facebook.com/ginvaughanbooks.

Blessings!
Virginia

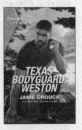